camp CONFIDENTIAL

D0064401

Extra Credit

GROSSET & DUNLAP
Published by the Penguin Group
Penguin Group (USA) Inc., 375 Hudson Street, New York,
New York 10014, USA
Penguin Group (Canada), 90 Eglinton Avenue East, Suite 700, Toronto,
Ontario M4P 2Y3, Canada (a division of Pearson Penguin Canada Inc.)
Penguin Books Ltd., 80 Strand, London WC2R 0RL, England
Penguin Group Ireland, 25 St. Stephen's Green, Dublin 2, Ireland
(a division of Penguin Books Ltd.)
Penguin Group (Australia), 250 Camberwell Road, Camberwell, Victoria
3124, Australia (a division of Pearson Australia Group Pty. Ltd.)
Penguin Books India Pvt. Ltd., 11 Community Centre, Panchsheel Park,
New Delhi—110 017, India
Penguin Group (NZ), 67 Apollo Drive, Rosedale, North Shore 0632,
New Zealand (a division of Pearson New Zealand Ltd.)
Penguin Books (South Africa) (Pty.) Ltd., 24 Sturdee Avenue,
Rosebank, Johannesburg 2196, South Africa

Penguin Books Ltd., Registered Offices:
80 Strand, London WC2R 0RL, England

If you purchased this book without a cover, you should be aware that this
book is stolen property. It was reported as "unsold and destroyed" to
the publisher, and neither the author nor the publisher has received any
payment for this "stripped book."

The scanning, uploading, and distribution of this book via the Internet or
via any other means without the permission of the publisher is illegal and
punishable by law. Please purchase only authorized electronic editions,
and do not participate in or encourage electronic piracy of copyrighted
materials. Your support of the author's rights is appreciated.

Cover design by Ching N. Chan
Front cover images © Digital Vision Photography/Veer Incorporated

Text copyright © 2009 by Penguin Group (USA) Inc. All rights reserved.
Published by Grosset & Dunlap, a division of Penguin Young Readers Group,
345 Hudson Street, New York, New York 10014. GROSSET & DUNLAP is a
trademark of Penguin Group (USA) Inc. Printed in the U.S.A.

Library of Congress Control Number: 2009012869

ISBN 978-0-448-45216-6   10 9 8 7 6 5 4 3 2 1

camp CONFIDENTIAL

Extra Credit

by Melissa J. Morgan

Grosset & Dunlap

chapter ONE

Posted by: Natalie
Subject: who wants to be a supahstah?

or superstar if you're doing normal-speak.
brynn, i can see you stretching your hand toward the
ceiling and me-me-me-ing even though I haven't
given any of the deets yet. take a breath. good. now
read on. this director friend of my dad's is shooting
a movie in guilford, ct, and she needs a ton of
high school extras. the movie is this time travel
thriller where sam quinn is searching for his lost son
through all these different time periods. i guess some
evil genius physicist has snatched the kid and is
holding him hostage in some other time—but in the
same place, his school. something about time being
bendable and . . . please don't make me explain it. it
will make my head hurt and i have a spanish test . . .
er . . . whatever the spanish word for tomorrow is.
see? thinking about traveling through time but
staying in the same place has wiped my brain.

some ammo for parents that need convincing: the director has a daughter of her own about our age and is all about the importance of school and bedtime and all that, so she's only shooting the big scenes with all the kid extras on weekends. if you want in, all you gotta do is show up at 8943 stockton ave two weeks from saturday at ten. you'll get the rest of the schedule then.

love you! mean it!

Natalie was so glad the Camp Lakeview blog hadn't shut down when the camp had. It had just kind of morphed into the Lakeviewalla blog. It was mostly Lakeview girls—make that former-Lakeview-now-Walla-Walla girls—but with a few old-time Camp Walla Walla girls mixed in. Like Avery, who had been one of Natalie, Jenna, Sloan, Chelsea, Brynn, and Priya's tentmates over the summer.

For most of the summer it had seemed like there was absolutely nothing in Avery to like, but she'd turned out to have a hidden streak of actual niceness. Living with her reminded Natalie of the first summer with Chelsea. And Chelsea had ended up a friend, too.

If Avery decided she wanted to be an extra, it would actually be sort of cool. Natalie was almost positive she could count on getting in some Brynn time. She figured Brynn would do anything to get her parents' permission to be in the movie—hunger strike, nonstop Shakespeare recitations at full volume. She might even get one of her drama club girls to impersonate her while she snuck off to Connecticut. Natalie smiled at the thought of Brynn coaching someone to act like her. Impossible. There was nobody quite like Brynn.

Posted by: Brynn
Subject: . . .

. . . .
That's me being speechless. You guys, I'm speechless. Have you ever seen—I mean heard—me speechless before? I don't think so. But when I read Nat's post, my voice got sucked right out of me. Seriously, I had to drink a glass of grapefruit juice—which, ewww—to remoisturize my mouth so I could ask my parents if I could be a supahstah. They weren't thrilled with me commuting two and a half hours to Guilford, but I told them I could use the train time for homework, and now I'm going to be in a movie! Yes, yes, yes! Yes!
Promise I'll remember I knew you when.

Posted by: Sarah
Subject: McSwoony

Sam Quinn is in the movie. Sam. Quinn.
I am so there.

Posted by: Jenna
Subject: McOldy

Sarah, it must be said. Sam Quinn is old. Can't wait to see my Walla Walla/Lakeview girls on the big screen!

P.S. *Mañana*. That's the word you're looking for, Nat. Say it after me. *Mañana*.

Posted by: Brynn
Subject: Thinkless

I was thinkless as well as speechless when I posted before. I forgot to ask who else is going to join me in stardom. Nat, you're going to be in the movie, right? NYC is closer to Guilford than Boston is.

What about you, Pree? We could meet up on the train. I know drama isn't especially your thing, but it'll be fuuun being an extra. Avery? You're right in Connecticut? You in?

Sarah, no swooning over McSwoony. Being an extra is a professional gig! (Well, you can swoon on the inside.)

Posted by: Priya
Subject: Bike Marathon

Jordan and I entered this bike marathon. It's not for a month and a half, but I have to train. There is no way that boy is beating me.

This will probably be my last post for a month and a half. Talk to you all after I kick behind!

Posted by: Brynn
Subject: Jordan's behind

No kicking, Pree! I like my bf's behind the way it is!

Posted by: Sloan
Subject: Outlook Good

I've consulted the tarot, the *I Ching*, the leaves in the cup of tea I just drank, and, of course, the Magic 8 Ball. All revealed a happy outcome for the extras in the movie. Go for it! The Sedona girl knows all. =)

Natalie grinned as she read Sloan's post. Of course being an extra was going to be a happy outcome. Natalie wasn't a drama girl like Brynn or a Sam Quinn megafan like Sarah, but hanging out on a movie set with her buds—what could be bad about that?

Posted by: Natalie
Subject: Outlook Fantabulous

i'm not from sedona, center of all things mystical. But i am from nyc, and new yorkers know everything. i say the outlook for the extras is more than good. it's good squared. (see, i know math. told you nyc-ers know it all!)

can't wait to see some of my camp girls in a couple weeks!!

j'adore (i know french, too! well, perfume french.)

chapter
TWO

Avery couldn't help letting out a little snort as she read Natalie's latest post. New Yorkers always acted so superior. Didn't they have noses? Their city stank. It really did. Hot, rank air wafted up from the grates over the subways. There was always garbage on the streets. Not just scraps of paper, either. Food. Chicken bones and chewing gum. Yuck.

It was a fine place to visit. To go shopping. Maybe to see a play or go to a museum. But no human being should want to live there. Not when there were places like Connecticut so close by.

Avery decided there was no reason to put her thoughts in her post. She was sensitive like that.

Posted by: Avery
Subject: Unbelievable

No being an extra for this girl. But I'll be first

in line to see the rest of you. Now can we talk about something else, please . . . ?

Like, my birthday, for instance? It's coming up (hint, hint—when you're mailing presents you have to buy early!) and I'm pretty sure I know what I'm getting from my dad and the new(ish) wife. I was going through my father's briefcase because I needed a pen—and because I wanted to find clues about my b-day present—and I found all these paint chips and carpet samples.

It looks like I'm finally getting my room redecorated. What else can it be, right? I've been dropping hint bombs for my dad all over the place, keeping the TV on decorating shows 24/7, plus leaving decorating mags in my father's office, open to pages with my picks for bedding and curtains and furniture. I want the extreme makeover. I hope my father realizes that means a lot more than a bed-in-a-bag. I want a new bed, too! And a revamped closet. And a window se—

To be continued. My worse half—the twin—is invading. And obnoxiously reading over my shoulder.

She quickly logged off the computer, twisted around in her desk chair, and shot her best evil eye at her brother, Peter.

He laughed. "Like there is anything worth keeping secret in your little camp blog. I loooove Sam Quinn. I want to have a million of his babies."

"You've watched all his movies about a million

times," Avery reminded him. She'd been so happy when he'd gotten his own DVD player. Not that she hadn't won most of the what-to-watch fights with Peter. But still . . .

"Yeah, but I don't watch them because I looove him," Peter answered. He flopped down on her bed. "I hope Dad and Elise don't think decorating is an acceptable birthday present for *me*." He picked up a heart-shaped pillow and tossed it at her.

Avery caught it. "You haven't been hinting. You have to hint to get what you want. It's clearly worked for me—as you learned from your snoopage."

"Going through Dad's briefcase wasn't snoopage?" Peter asked.

"That was snooping to find out something about *me*," Avery told him. Peter could be a teeny bit dense. "You were just snooping to snoop."

"I really came in to see if you'd bogied the chocolate chip cookies," Peter said.

"They're gone? I haven't even eaten one," Avery answered. "You should ask Elise. Have you noticed she's been getting a little puffy?" Avery was actually hoping Elise would be forced to admit that her blue silk shirt was now too small—and give it to Avery.

"Yeah. She'd better watch it. I think there's a strict weight limit on trophy wives." Peter shoved himself off the bed.

Avery raised one eyebrow. "Trophy wife. You think she ever qualified?" Elise was pretty, Avery had to give her that. But trophy pretty? Um, no.

Peter shrugged as he headed out the door. Avery

logged back on to the computer. Maybe she could find a few good shopping links to send her dad. She really didn't want to have to endure a bed-in-a-bag fiasco on her birthday.

▲ ▲ ▲

"Now I'll definitely get a boyfriend," the girl sitting next to Natalie—she'd said her name was Jo—went on.

Shut up, Natalie thought. *Please, shut up, shut up, shut up.*

"Maybe I'll even ask out this guy, Noah, at school. I've had a crush on him since sixth grade. In sixth grade, there were only two guys it was acceptable to like—Noah Snyder or John Martin. That's it. If you asked any girl, they would always say one or the other."

Please, just stop talking, Natalie silently begged. But Jo just kept going. And going. And going.

"I didn't like him just because you had to like one of them, though," she went on. "I really liked him-liked him. And I still do. And I think without these—" Jo gestured to her mouth "—maybe he might like me, too. It's Friday. Maybe I'll just text him and see what he's doing this weekend. I should just go for it, don't you think?"

Natalie gave a sort of nod, sort of head shake and picked up a magazine. It was two years old. She started to read it, anyway. Jo kept talking.

"I'm going to join the debate team, too. I've always been good at coming up with the arguments, but I never wanted to join because—" Out of the corner of her eye, Natalie caught Jo gesturing to her mouth again. "I just hated having people look at me. How could they even listen to what I was saying with—" her hand waved at her mouth yet again "—with this face full of junk?"

Natalie started flicking through the magazine. She couldn't concentrate enough to read with Jo going on and on and on.

"Yeah, I'm definitely going to call Noah today," Jo went on.

"Good idea." Natalie tossed the magazine down on the table. "I hope you find out it was your braces that were keeping him away from you before, and not something like your—"

Natalie stopped herself before she said the word "personality," but Jo's eyes still widened with hurt. "I'm sorry," Natalie said. "It's just that I'm getting braces *on*. Listening to how happy you are about getting them off is kind of hard."

Jo reached out and put her hand on Natalie's wrist. "That was really selfish of me. I'm just so . . ."

"Happy," Natalie finished for her, then sighed. "It's cool to be happy. I'm sure I'll be happy when I get mine off. Someday."

"I would say it's not so bad, but I kind of think you might not believe me," Jo said.

Natalie gave a bark of laughter. "Probably not," she agreed.

"I'm trying to think of *something* good I can say." A long, icky silence stretched out. "The orthodontist's assistant is pretty cute, so you'll have something nice to stare at."

"With my mouth hanging open," Natalie added.

"Still," Jo said.

"Jo Womsley," the receptionist called.

"That's me." Jo stood up. "Sorry about . . . you know."

"It's okay," Natalie answered. It's not like she wouldn't have found out soon enough that her life was totally, completely, utterly over.

Not forever, she told herself. *Just for the next two years!*

To: NatalieNYC, SarahSports
From: BrynnWins
Re: What our lives could be

I know I'm the drama girl, but I don't think I'm being dramatic when I say that our lives could totally change starting tomorrow. Nat, you were joking around—at least I thought you were—when you asked who wanted to be a superstar, but all three of us could be. Check out this article I found about Ember Davis. Did you know she started out as an extra??? An extra—as in what we're going to be tomorrow!

Check it.

EMBER ON FIRE

Ember Davis has just been cast as Ferris Bueller in the remake of '80s classic Ferris Bueller's Day Off. *Director Camden Perry said he wasn't considering changing the lead from male to female until he saw Davis in her breakout role of Geebee in* Wonderworld. *Most think that was Davis's first film credit, but two years before she was in* The Lost Farm. *Davis was an extra in the film, but was moved up to a featured extra by director Zan Lazarus, who was struck by "the way her personality shone out of her face."*

There's a lot more, but that's the part I wanted you to see. And you know who is directing our movie. Nat, I know you know. But Sarah, in case you don't, it's Zan Lazarus!! She could pull us out of obscurity, too. (Not that you're exactly in obscurity, Natalie. You're the daughter of Oscar-nominee Tad Maxwell—don't you have to say Oscar-nominee every time you say his name now?)

See you tomorrow—when our new lives begin!!!

-Brynn

chapter

THREE

"Sarah, over here!" Brynn frantically waved her arms over her head to get Sarah's attention. It was all she could do to restrain herself from bouncing. Bouncing wasn't professional extra behavior, and Brynn intended to be professional.

"This is the line to get costumes," she said when Sarah reached her.

"Are you planning on camping out?" Sarah asked, nodding at the two large duffel bags at Brynn's feet. "I know it's a long way out here, but—"

"It would almost be easier to camp, right?" Brynn answered. "But this—" she nudged one of the duffels with her toes "—is all stuff to help us be better extras. On this movie, they're handling wardrobe. Sometimes extras do that themselves. But we still might need to look different from scene to scene, so I borrowed some wigs and glasses from the drama department at school. Also, I brought my tap shoes, a yo-yo, a harmonica, a baseball glove—"

"What? Why did you lug all that junk here?" Sarah interrupted.

"Sometimes there might be a need for a special skill on the set. I wanted to be prepared. Because if you and your skill get used—even in the background—you get a SAG voucher." Brynn realized she was talking faster than she usually did, too fast to really enunciate even, but she couldn't slow down. Even her tongue was excited about being on a movie set! "If you get three of the vouchers, you get to be a member of SAG."

"I feel a 'huh' coming. Yeah, here it is. Huh? SAG?" Sarah repeated.

"Screen Actors Guild. It's a union. You can't be a professional actor unless you're a member of SAG." Brynn looked down at her duffels. "I also brought some magazines—with quizzes—because being an extra involves a *lot* of waiting. I'm going to try and spend the downtime networking, but I thought you and Nat might want them."

"All I brought was lunch. And some homework. But I got most of it done on the train," Sarah said.

"Food's a good idea, although they'll feed us. But there are always long lines," Brynn answered.

"Okay, tell me. How many hours have you spent Googling to find out all this stuff?" Sarah asked.

"Uh, how many hours has it been since Natalie sent out that post?" Brynn asked.

Sarah laughed. "That's what I thought. Speaking of Miss Natalie . . ."

"I know. Where is she? Being late is a complete extra no-no." Brynn looked down the line, then across the wide, green quad that stretched out on either side of it. The movie—at least this part of the movie—was shooting on a college campus that was standing in for a boarding school—the school Sam Quinn's son was supposed to go to. A lot of the movie took place there because Sam Quinn was searching for his son at the school in several different time periods.

Brynn squinted her eyes—no Natalie.

"I'm going to call her." Brynn pulled out her cell. "Hey, Nat. It's Brynn and Sarah. We're in line to get fitted for our costumes, and you're not. Where are you?"

"The fun can't start until you get here!" Sarah called out in the background.

"See you soon, we hope," Brynn added, then hung up.

"Some of Nat's shoes aren't designed for fast walking," Sarah pointed out. "Or even walking at all. That could explain the lateness."

"True," Brynn agreed. "Although every pair she wears gives me shoe envy." She and Sarah shuffled a few feet closer to the gym/wardrobe center entrance. "So you want some other extra tips? They'll make you the equivalent of an old camper."

"Then definitely," Sarah answered.

"All right, let's go over some vocab. The honeywagon is a trailer with changing rooms and a bathroom. It's not a place for food, even though it sounds like it should be."

"Honey doesn't equal food. Got it," Sarah said.

"You don't start acting—you know, doing your

background stuff—when the director says 'action.' You start when she—our director is a she, which is cool—or the assistant director says 'background.' "

Sarah nodded. "Background, because we're in the background. Makes sen—"

"I don't know any of that. But I do know where the snack shack is set up. Actually, it's not a snack shack. It's more like a Starbucks in a tent." A voice interrupted the girls' conversation. Brynn jerked her head toward the direction of the voice—and saw a cute boy, make that *very* cute, smiling at Sarah. Brynn looked over at Sarah, waiting for an intro. She figured Sarah must know the guy from school. In fact, Brynn wondered if she herself knew him as well. There was something awfully familiar about his face.

"Come on," Very Cute Boy urged. "I can tell you need a caramel macchiato." He turned to Brynn. "Look at her eyes. Don't you think it's almost gotten to be a medical condition? That's what my stepmom calls it when she needs caffeine—a medical condition. I just like caramel."

Brynn looked at Sarah's eyes, which were wide with surprise. Brynn started to think that maybe Sarah had never seen V.C.B. before. "Uh, well, we're getting pretty close to the front of the line . . ." Brynn said.

"But the coffee is very close," V.C.B. said. "And we'll get one for you, too. You're reaching a medical crisis yourself. I can see it. So you save our place, and Sarah and I will go get coffee."

"How do you know my name?" Sarah asked.

Yup, Brynn was right. V.C.B. was also A.T.S. A Total Stranger.

"I know it by basically eavesdropping," V.C.B./A.T.S. admitted. "My name is Chace Turner, since you didn't have the chance to eavesdrop on me. Not that either of you would eavesdrop. I'm sure you're much too nice for that."

Brynn was glad he told them his name. All the initials she'd assigned him were getting confusing.

"So you can save our place, uh—" Chace hesitated. "I wasn't eavesdropping long enough to hear your name."

"Brynn," Sarah told him.

Chace's smile widened. "Brynn. So Brynn will save our place in line and we'll get her—" He glanced at Brynn, who glanced at Sarah, trying to figure out what her friend wanted to do.

"Some coffee would be good," Sarah said. Which was code for "he's cute enough for you to leave me alone with him."

"Mochachino," Brynn said, and without another word, Chace and Sarah were off. Brynn stared after them. She felt a little like she had brain whiplash.

▲ ▲ ▲

Sarah felt a little like she had what Brynn would call brain whiplash. She'd been standing in line with Brynn, basically getting a vocabulary lesson. And now she was walking across the green lawn of a college campus, past a big, gurgling fountain, with this guy who looked almost too cute to be real.

What had just happened?

It's not that she'd never had a guy notice her. She'd had boyfriends, even. Yeah, her very first summer at Lakeview, Sarah had been one of the girls who had zero interest in boys. But she'd definitely grown out of that.

This was different, though. There were tons of girls here today. Lots of the glam wannabe-actress kind of girls. But this guy Chace had walked right up to her. It's not like he knew anything about her. That he wanted to hang with her because he liked the same books she liked or was a Red Sox fan, too. Sarah peeked at him out of the corner of her eye. *Why me?* she thought.

"Sam Quinn is paying for the coffee tent," Chace told her. "How cool is that? He's this megastar, and he's shelling out for coffee for everybody, even us extras. I guess I kind of think of big stars as being in their own worlds, not thinking of anything but themselves. But it turns out they can be pretty cool, huh?" He winked at her.

Winking . . . that was a pretty cheesy move. Right up there with using your fingers as guns. It looked good on Chace, though. There probably wasn't much that didn't look good on him. He was almost impossibly good looking, but in a very familiar sort of way.

"It was cool of him to give free coffee to everyone." Sarah could smell the coffee now, and when they rounded the corner past the library, she could see the tent. It was huge, red and yellow striped, with people all around, talking and laughing.

"Yeah, especially because I bet he had to take a hammer to his piggy bank," Chace joked as they joined the line. "So was I right about you? Are you a caramel macchiato girl?"

"Um, yep, that's me," Sarah answered. Actually, she was more of a Gatorade girl. Orange juice, grape juice, apple juice, even bug juice. Or soda. She'd only had coffee once and she didn't like it. She liked the smell, but not the taste. How could she say that now, though? She'd come over here with Chace to get *coffee*, and wasn't coffee more, well, adult than the other stuff?

"Me too. Except a guy. I'm a caramel macchiato guy," Chace quickly added, and they both laughed.

"Yeah, I realized the guy part," Sarah told him.

"Ah. A smart girl. I like," Chace said.

"And I like a guy who eavesdrops," Sarah teased. "I don't think I said anything smart when you were eavesdropping."

Chace winced. "I should never have admitted that. I should have said I was psychic. Or that you just looked like a Sarah or something."

They reached the front of the line and Chace ordered their coffees. Chace handed Sarah hers, and then he stared at her for a minute. Sarah began feeling kind of jittery. What was he staring at?

"You have caramel macchiato eyes," he said. Then he snorted. "I can't believe that came out of my mouth. I sounded like a total cheeseball. But I just noticed that your eyes are really awesome."

Awesome was a little much. Sarah had seen her eyes a million times. They were just your basic brown.

"They really are the same color as caramel macchiatos. But in the center, around the pupil, there's a slightly darker ring." Chace leaned in so close that Sarah could feel his warm breath against her face. Sarah didn't feel like *she* could breathe at all. She wanted to back away and, at the same time, she had this impulse to close the small distance between them. So she stayed exactly where she was.

"No, not a ring exactly," Chace continued. "The edges aren't smooth. It's more like a starburst. And actually, the outside of your eye does have a ring—a smooth, perfect ring, of the same darker color, all around it."

No boy had every looked at her this way. This closely. This intensely.

Her ex-boyfriend David would have cracked up if he'd tried to stare into her eyes this long. *She* would have cracked up.

But Sarah didn't feel like laughing now. Actually, she felt kind of dizzy. Kind of dazed. Kind of . . . crushed.

▲ ▲ ▲

Natalie walked into the four-story townhouse mansion that was the Henri Bendel department store. She thought maybe one of their signature brown and white bags might cheer her up a little.

Bendel's wasn't one of her usual shopping spots, but it felt right for what her mom called "retail therapy." It was so elegant, so completely New York. But standing there surrounded by the glossy, dark-wood makeup counters, Natalie wasn't feeling her happiness meter go up.

What she was feeling was her teeth aching from the new braces. What she was feeling was an unwillingness to open her mouth and let the junk on her teeth be seen. What she was feeling was miserable.

Maybe she needed more than the cosmetics and candles on the first floor. She loved new makeup, but maybe this round of retail therapy required more serious shopping. Natalie climbed the curving staircase, with its black wrought iron railing, up to the second floor—fashion, jewelry, and fragrance.

The Memoire Liquide section caught her eye. The shelves held more than one hundred old-fashioned, little bottles with stoppers. Each one contained a perfume oil, and the oils could be combined into a bespoke perfume, a perfume that was made especially for you.

Natalie had been wanting to get her own perfume made for a long time. Maybe today was the day. A specialist would help her select the oils, and then Memoire Liquide would keep her perfume recipe on file so she could buy more whenever she wanted it.

She took a step toward the rows of little bottles waiting for her, then hesitated. She didn't really feel like talking. At all. And she wouldn't be able to concoct her perfume without talking to the specialist a little. Plus, the whole point of the perfume was to reflect your personality and emotions. Natalie didn't think she wanted to smell the way she was feeling right now.

Instead, she veered over to one of the fashion areas. It *was* soothing, the new smell everywhere, all the clothes perfectly folded or hung neatly. She found an Alice + Olivia tank dress with a cute ruffled and embroidered hem. Her size, too. As she took it off the rack, her cell rang.

It was Brynn. Again. Natalie still didn't feel like talking, but if she didn't pick up, Brynn would probably send out a search and rescue team. She sighed, punched Talk, and said, "Hi, Brynn."

"That's not what you say. You say, 'Brynn, I'm stuck on the train' or 'Brynn, I'm in the emergency room because I chipped the polish on my big toe!' "

"I'm sorry. I should have called you and Sarah before," Natalie answered. "I'm just not in the mood for the extras thing."

"In the mood?" Brynn's voice went up an octave with each word. "It's not like people get this chance every day. Did you read that article I sent—the one about Ember Davis? This could be our start. And I know you *say* acting isn't your thing, but I also know that you were all ready to go to that improv class your dad wanted you to take before we all decided on Walla Walla this summer."

Natalie caught sight of herself in one of the store's many mirrors and flashed a sarcastic smile. *Yes, that would look lovely on-screen*, she thought. *I'm sure anyone who saw me would immediately realize I should be a star just like my dad.*

"Nat. Hello? I know you'd be late if you left now. But your dad knows the director and everything. You can still come. Opportunity of a lifetime," Brynn coaxed.

"Not really. At least not for me," Natalie answered, saying the first thing she could think of to get Brynn off the phone. "My dad can get me an actual part in a movie any time I want one. I don't really have to start as an extra."

She'd just come off as exactly the kind of movie star's kid she hated. But no other excuse had come into her head, so she rolled with it.

"Oh. Okay," Brynn told her. "Yeah, of course, that makes sense."

She sounded hurt. Why wouldn't she? Natalie had basically just given her an I'm-better-than-you smackdown. "You and Sarah have fun, though," Natalie quickly added. "And I want to hear everything."

"Me and Sarah, right," Brynn answered. "She completely ditched me for this cute boy. Okay, this very cute boy."

A very cute boy, Natalie thought. *Wonder when one of those will ever look at me again.*

"Why don't you come hang out with me? I have magazines. With quizzes," Brynn bribed.

"I can't. I'm shopping. Go become a star. I know you will," Natalie said, then hung up before Brynn could reply. She rushed into the nearest changing room with her dress. She needed this retail therapy to kick in *stat*.

Natalie shimmied out of her clothes and slid on the silky tank dress. Cute. And with her lime pumps, very cute. From the chin down.

She yanked the dress off over her head and dropped it to the floor. What was she doing? The point of a cute dress was to get people—especially boy people—to notice you. And if anyone noticed her right now, it wouldn't take them very long to see the horror show that was her mouth.

Natalie left the elegant store as quickly as she could without breaking into a run.

chapter

FOUR

Go slower, Brynn silently ordered the wardrobe line. In about three steps she would be inside the wardrobe area—and Sarah and Chace still weren't back. She wasn't going to be able to hold their places much longer. *Go slower, line.*

Clearly her mind-control powers were being jammed by evil forces, because two seconds later the line jerked forward. Brynn took one . . . two . . . three . . . four steps. And she was through the doorway to the gym. She peered behind her, hoping to catch a glimpse of Sarah and Chace, the now-more-annoying-than-cute boy, running toward her. But no.

And the line kept on moving. Two more steps and she could almost reach out and touch one of the dozens of rolling racks of costumes. Which was so cool. Except Sarah wasn't here. Natalie, either.

What was with Natalie, anyway? Brynn wondered. Her friend had practically hung up on her, and that was after going all my-daddy's-a-movie-star-and-can-get-me-anything-I-want, which so wasn't Nat.

A lot of the time, Natalie didn't even tell people she was Tad Maxwell's daughter right off. Like at Walla Walla during the summer, Nat hadn't told any of the girls who didn't already know her from Camp Lakeview about her dad. In fact, Sarah had told her whole tent that Tad Maxwell was *her* father, and the truth didn't come out until the end of the summer, because Natalie didn't go around talking about how she was movie star spawn. So how come Nat had—

"You're up, petunia," a twenty-something girl called to Brynn, pulling her away from her thoughts about Natalie's bizarre behavior.

Brynn hurried over to her. "Hi, I'm Brynn. I'm an extra, but, duh, you know that, because here I am." Brynn's tongue had slipped into excited overdrive again. Her feet, too. She couldn't help giving a couple toe bounces. "Is my hair okay? Because it could be a different color. With wigs. From in there." She pointed to one of her duffel bags.

The girl laughed. "Hey, Brynn. I'm Dax, one of the wardrobe assistants. And your hair is fine. Beautiful, actually. I love red hair." She started flipping through a rack of pants. "You really brought wigs?"

Brynn nodded, biting her tongue. She didn't want to start another babblefest. So *not* professional.

"Good call. Most first-timers don't know to do that, but sometimes we do need different hair on people for different scenes. Or maybe just because an extra's hair is too similar to one of the stars'," Dax commented.

Brynn flushed, a little out of embarrassment, a little out of pleasure. Embarrassment because it had been so completely obvious to Dax that Brynn was a first-time extra. Pleasure because she'd made the right move—the professional move—by bringing the wigs.

"I'm thinking these." Dax handed Brynn a pair of hip-hugging brown corduroy pants with huge bell bottoms. "With this." She turned to another rack and grabbed a crocheted vest with a yellow, green, and purple butterfly on the back, then added a thin, purple turtleneck. "Now you need shoes. I'm going to get you a pair of Famolares. Everybody your age—well, girls— was wearing them in the '70s. The soles had these big, funky waves that were supposed to be good for—"

"Hey!" a guy loudly protested from behind them, interrupting Dax. "There's a line."

Brynn looked over her shoulder and saw Sarah and Chace hurrying toward her. "She's saving our place," Chace told Protesting Guy.

"That's not fair," a girl complained. "The rest of us have been standing here the whole time."

"She's right," Dax told Chace and Sarah. "Sorry, sugarpops, but you two have to go to the back. Although . . ." She peered at the line stretching out the door. "It might be better just to come back tomorrow. We only need about ten more extras for the scene we're shooting today. There's really no chance you'll get used."

"But we just went to get Brynn coffee so she

could get rid of her migraine." Chace thrust a large paper coffee cup into Brynn's hands. "Caffeine's the only thing that works on them. And she didn't want to go home. Being an extra is all she's been talking about for the last week."

"That's true," Brynn agreed. That part really was true.

Dax hesitated. "Fine. I guess you two shouldn't be penalized for being good friends," she finally told Sarah and Chace. "I'll get you outfitted next."

Chace turned to Brynn. "Drink that. You're probably about two seconds away from seeing those flashing lights. She sees these weird auras right before the headache really hits. Then she pukes," Chace explained to Dax.

He sounded like he'd known her for years and had helped her through a dozen migraines. His face was full of concern, like all he cared about was making sure she wasn't in pain. *You are a very good liar, Chace,* she thought.

"And . . . background!" the assistant director called.

Brynn used the mirror inside "her" locker to brush her hair, ignoring the camera, ignoring the crew. She was a '70s high school girl, and she was brushing her hair because she had to give an oral report in her next class.

The assistant director, or AD as the pros say, had told her to stand at the locker and brush her hair, but he hadn't come up with the backstory about the oral report. Brynn had developed that herself. A girl didn't brush her hair the same way to get ready for a class assignment as she did if she knew she was going to see a guy she liked, and a real actress had to know what was going on in her character's head. Brynn thought that should apply even if your character was just somebody in the background of a scene. She'd decided her character's name was Dawn because her mom had an old friend named Dawn. They'd gone to high school together in the '70s, so it seemed like a good '70s name.

"And cut!" the AD called. "Looked great, everybody! Now we're going to add Sam Quinn to the scene. You'll be doing what you've been doing, and Sam will come running down the hall, searching for his son. Definitely look at him. He's going to be panic-stricken, in a sweat, yelling. So it would be weird if you didn't look. Just look at him like a crazy parent, not like a movie star, okay?"

Brynn nodded, trying to imagine how Dawn would react to an agitated parent running down the hall. Would she be annoyed that he was distracting her from her oral report? Worried? Did Dawn know the son he was looking for?

"Hang loose. I'll let you know when we're ready to get started," the AD added. Then he headed over to confer with the director.

Brynn left her locker and walked over to Sarah and Chace. They were part of a group of kids who came piling out of the classroom door near Brynn's locker as soon as "background" was called.

"You're finally going to see your buddy Sam Quinn," Brynn joked to Sarah.

Sarah gave her head a tiny shake, and Brynn immediately understood. Sarah didn't want Brynn talking about Sarah's celebrity crush in front of her new real-life crush, so Brynn did a quick subject change. "That stuff I read online was so right about the amount of waiting in the life of an extra."

It had taken hours to do four takes of the hallway background. First the assistant director had to give them all their instructions, then there were long delays between each take while the lighting was changed for new camera angles. Brynn had kept an eye out for networking opportunities, but everyone on the crew seemed really busy. Trying to network with someone who was trying to work was a definite extra no-no.

"For this break, I suggest we play Rock, Paper, Scissors, Algebra, Dead Fish," Chace said. He'd elected himself social coordinator, coming up with something for the little group in their part of the hallway to do during all their downtime.

Sarah laughed. "Whoa, back up a second? Dead fish?"

"It's this new version I came up with. Algebra destroys paper. Paper wraps dead fish. Scissors cut off dead fish's head. Rock smashes—

"Oh, I get it," Brynn interrupted. "It's like the version they play on *The Big Bang Theory*. Rock, Paper, Scissors, Lizard, Spock. Lizard poisons Spock. Spock vaporizes rock. Something destroys Spock."

"Paper disproves Spock," a redheaded guy named Lowell said. "I love that show."

"I never watch it," Chace told him. "I guess great minds just think alike."

Brynn noticed a slight flush creeping up the back of Chace's neck. She was almost positive he was lying. Again. In *The Big Bang Theory* version of the game, scissors cut off lizard's head, just like how Chace's scissors cut off a dead fish's head. Great minds didn't think *that* much alike. Did they?

She didn't have much time to explore that thought before the AD called all the extras back to their places.

Back in character, Brynn opened her locker and picked up her hairbrush. *You're Dawn now*, she reminded herself as she waited for the AD to call "background."

She heard one of the assistants call out the scene number and then the AD called out, "Background!" Brynn started brushing the flip one of the stylists had given her. As she brushed, she reviewed her tips for her oral report: Stand up straight, make eye contact, but not with Adam because he always made her laugh, breathe after every—

Footsteps pounded down the hallway, and Brynn automatically jerked toward the sound. Sam Quinn was racing along the hall, sweat making a wet V on the front of his T-shirt. "Gabriel!" he shouted. "I know you're here, buddy. Show me where you are, and I'll get you out of here. I'll get you home."

"Cut!" This time it was Zan making the call.

She walked over to Sam Quinn and they had a low conversation. Then Zan strode right over to Brynn's little cluster of extras!

"You guys are doing a great job," she told them. "What's your name, Red?" she asked, nodding toward Lowell.

"Matthews. Lowell Matthews," he answered quickly.

Zan grinned. "Clearly a fan of Bond, James Bond," she said. "Me too. So, Lowell, what I want you to do is head for the drinking fountain when you come out of the classroom with the rest of the group." She gestured toward the fountain almost directly opposite where Brynn and the rest of the extras were standing. "But before you get there, I want you to kneel down and tie your shoe—so untie it now."

"Got it," Lowell said, his eyes bright with excitement. Brynn didn't blame him—she would be excited, too. Zan had just positioned him right in the middle of the action. That was prime location for an extra. Lowell would definitely get some screen time.

"This is important. Once you kneel down, stay down. Sam is going to jump over you." Sam must have heard his name because he turned and waved. "You won't get hurt as long as you just stay still, okay, Mr. Bond?"

"Okay," Lowell told her.

Zan started back toward Sam, then turned around. "Oh, I want you to say, 'Smooth move, Six Million Dollar Man,' after he makes the jump. Just to emphasize that it's the '70s. Let me hear it."

Lowell said the line with just the right amount of wow-ness. "Great," Zan said. "I want to rehearse it one time," she called to the AD.

"You just earned yourself a SAG voucher," Brynn told Lowell. "Two more of those and you get to be a member of the Screen Actors Guild. You're on your way to being a professional!"

"That's so awesome," said Temple, an extra with two long, hippie-style ponytails and lots of love beads.

"Really?" Lowell turned to Chace for confirmation.

Chace didn't seem to have heard him for a minute. His face was completely blank.

"Chace?" Sarah said.

"Yeah! Definitely! One down, two to go!" Chace finally answered. He gave Lowell an overenthusiastic slap on the shoulder. "Nice going!"

To Brynn it sounded like he was trying a little too hard to sound happy for Lowell. Which was another kind of lying, wasn't it?

▲ ▲ ▲

"I was really proud of you today," Brynn told Sarah as they waited in line to buy their train tickets home from Guilford. "You kept all your swooning on the inside."

"Oh, good," Sarah answered. "I've completely got the likes for Chace, even though I just met him. But he doesn't need to know that. At least that's what all the magazine articles—and Chelsea—say."

Brynn stared at her. "I wasn't talking about Chace. I was talking about your reason for being an extra in the first place—McSwoony himself. You didn't attempt to get an autograph. You didn't even stare at him, except when we were all supposed to be staring."

"I didn't stare. Just some peeking out of the corner of my eye," Sarah confessed. But truthfully, she hadn't really done much of that, either. Most of her attention had been focused on Chace. And every time she had looked over at him, he seemed to be looking back at her with his lake-colored eyes. "Don't you think his eyes are exactly the color of the lake at Camp Walla Walla?" she asked, bursting with enthusiasm.

"Well, I didn't stare, but I admit I did a little peeking, too," Brynn answered. "And I think his eyes are a lot more summer-sky blue." She paid for her train ticket, and then waited for Sarah to pay for hers. "I'd say we should get a soft pretzel or something while we wait for our trains, but they gave us waaay too much food on the set. How much do I enjoy saying that—on the set? So very much."

"Chace's eyes are definitely not blue," Sarah said as she led the way to a couple of empty seats in the waiting area. "They are green mixed with—"

"Chace? I thought we were talking about Sam 'McSwoony' Quinn."

Sarah gave a little frown. "Oh, yeah. I guess we were. But anyway, what did you think of him—Chace? He reminds me of someone, though. And I can't

40

quite put my finger on who."

And the way he kept finding little reasons to brush up against me, she silently added. Like when he adjusted her headband—for "continuity"—between shots in the movie. Or when he kept grabbing her hand so he could rub his fingers over her mood ring—part of her '70s costume—to see how he was feeling.

"I agree. He does have one of those faces that makes you think you've seen the person before," Brynn agreed. "And he's kind of a good liar," she added quickly.

"What are you talking about?" Sarah asked. She'd been with Chace every second Brynn had, and she hadn't heard Chace lie about anything.

"It was no big deal. It's just he came up with that story about me having a migraine and needing caffeine so fast," Brynn explained.

Sarah rolled her eyes. "That's hardly even lying. I mean, it's not a lie that hurt anyone or anything. Chace and I wouldn't have gotten to be extras today if he hadn't come up with it. I definitely wouldn't have thought of anything that fast."

"I guess that's what I meant. He's a good liar," Brynn said. "I didn't mean he was a bad person or anything."

"Chace wants to be an actor, just like you do," Sarah said. "Actors have to have great improv skills, right? That's what you saw—Chace being great at improv, not at lying."

"Yeah, you're right," Brynn agreed. "I didn't think of it like that. It was an impressive acting job."

Sarah nodded, satisfied. She wanted her friend to like Chace as much as she did. Well, no, not *as* much. But she wanted Brynn to like him. And she wanted him to like her friends. Because even though she'd only known him for one day, she had a feeling that Chace Turner was going to be somebody special in her life.

chapter
FIVE

Retail therapy had been a complete failure, so Natalie decided to spend Sunday in Central Park. Alone. Communicating with nature. Squirrels didn't really care if you had braces or not.

But squirrels weren't exactly great company, either.

Instead, Natalie chose a path that would take her by the little park zoo. She hadn't gone into the zoo in forever. There'd be some more entertaining animal friends in there. And she'd be by the zoo clock when the hour struck to see all the metal animals glide around the base of the clock. She'd get to see the hippopotamus with the violin. That had been her favorite for as long as she could remember.

Woo-hoo. I've really got an exciting day going, Natalie thought. *A metal hippo with a violin, a wide variety of live animals, maybe a bag of popcorn later.* Except popcorn was on the list of foods to avoid. Yup, Natalie had a list of foods to avoid now.

She wasn't supposed to eat anything hard or crunchy or sticky or chewy.

Natalie sighed as she headed toward the zoo's ticket booth. As she pulled out her wallet, someone tapped her on the shoulder. It was Colette, a girl from her language arts class.

"Hi, Nat. Are you here to do sketches for Ms. Furth's class? I've drawn my cat about a thousand times and I thought maybe I'd have better luck with a different animal. Although maybe my problem is lack of talent. I don't know why I signed up for art in the first place. I can hardly draw a stick figure."

"Not in art," Natalie mumbled, trying to speak without opening her mouth wide enough to show her braces.

"What?" Colette asked.

"Not taking art," Natalie said, speaking more loudly to force the words past her mostly closed lips. She thought she might have given Colette a little flash of braces, anyway.

"Oh. Okay."

Yeah, Colette had clearly seen the braces. She was acting all weird now. Usually Colette was really chatty. Now it was just "Oh. Okay."

"Are you going to get your ticket?" Colette asked.

Natalie definitely didn't want to walk around the zoo with Colette pretending that nothing was different about her. "Changed my mind," she muttered. She rushed off, and could feel Colette staring after her.

You're being paranoid, she told herself. But when she shot a quick glance over her shoulder, Colette really was staring, like Natalie was some kind of freak girl. Natalie jammed her hands in her jacket pockets and picked up her pace.

She walked without a destination, just wanting to *move*. A few minutes later, she passed the statue of Balto, the sled dog who had helped bring antitoxin serum across Alaska's icy tundra, saving the lives of hundreds of people. A little kid sat on Balto's back, as usual. Some kid was almost always getting his picture taken on top of Balto. In fact, the dog's back was shiny from all those kids' behinds sitting on him.

Natalie smiled, momentarily forgetting to keep her lips together. The breeze sent a chill through her metal braces, and an ache through her teeth. Her smile faded, and she kept walking.

She stopped at the Krebs Boathouse Café, just for something to do, and got a hot chocolate. Thank goodness she could still drink anything she wanted to! As she sipped, she watched the model boats glide over the small boat pond nearby. It was amazing to her how people got so into the little boats. Adult-type people, not little kids.

A guy around her age was the youngest person operating one of the remote control boats. He didn't go to her school. Natalie was pretty sure she wouldn't see anyone from her school around the pond. She didn't know anyone who was into model boats.

He's pretty cute, she thought. He had shaggy, blond hair. Not shaggy like he stood in front of a mirror with a can of mousse every morning, but shaggy like he didn't get it cut quite often enough. He definitely had emo bangs, without the emo vibe. And he had freckles. Just the right amount of freckles. Freckles as accessories, not as the dominant skin feature.

The boy turned toward her and caught her checking him out. He smiled, a kind of shy smile, a smile that showed a mouthful of braces. Natalie looked down, pretending that her hot chocolate required 110 percent of her attention.

Come on, Nat. Just yesterday you were wondering when a guy would look at you again. That boat boy is looking, she told herself. *So what are you going to do about it?*

Maybe "normal" boys wouldn't be interested in her until her mouth was no longer a construction zone. But that guy over there, who had just smiled at her, *he* had braces, too. So it made sense that her braces didn't repulse him.

Natalie stood up. Maybe she didn't have to be completely miserable. She finished her hot chocolate, tossed the cup in the trash, and walked over to the boy with the braces.

"Hi," she said.

He smiled again. "Hi."

"Nice boat," she told him.

"Want to try it?" he asked.

"Sure." They did the name exchange. He was Eli. Natalie liked that name.

"Have you ever sailed—either model or life-size?" Eli asked.

"I've gone out on a friend's boat a few times. But what I did was more lying around and sunning than sailing," Natalie admitted.

"Okay, then we have to go over the basics first," Eli said. "The wind's relationship to the sails is key to the motion of the boat.

"That much I did get as I was hanging out on deck," Natalie said.

"What you might not have known was that wind doesn't just push. The sails have a forward and a sideways pull, which makes the air deflect when it hits the sail. The air on the leeward side has a faster path than the air on the windward side. It's the difference in pressure that moves the boat forward. So figuring out—" Eli stopped and grimaced. "Just flick me on the forehead when I start getting all Bill Nye the Science Guy." He set the boat in the water and handed her the remote. "It will be more fun if you just play around with it. You'll figure out how to get the best speed."

"I won't tip it over or anything?" Natalie asked, her fingers poised on the controls.

"I built her and you're asking if she'll tip?" Eli asked, mock-insulted.

"Never mind, then." Natalie slid the lever on the remote forward, and the boat moved out into the pond. "So you made the boat from a kit?"

"No way. She's scratch built. I drew up the plans. I didn't let anybody else touch her. Just sanding the hull took forever. I used finer and finer grit down eight hundred wet sanding. Then I had to hose it off, use Turkish toweling rags, and then acetone . . . and this would probably be a good time for a forehead flick."

Natalie laughed. "I would, but my hands are full." She pressed the remote's lever to the left.

This was kinda fun. Eli was kinda fun. He was also kinda boring. All that tech talk about sideways pull and acetone . . .

But he liked hanging out with her. That was obvious. And it's not like she was going to have guys lining up to see her grotesque metallic smile.

"You want to exchange e-mails?" Natalie asked. She didn't like giving out her cell number right away.

Eli grinned so widely, the sun glinting off his braces was almost blinding. "Absolutely."

Presents next, Avery thought on Sunday night as she spotted a waiter heading toward their table carrying a chocolate cake loaded with candles—enough for her and Peter.

Yeah, yeah, she thought as her father, the stepmother, the waiter, and most of the people in the restaurant sang "Happy Birthday" to Avery and her twin. She was ready for her presents already!

She blew out all the candles without any help from Peter. Lately it was like he was always watching some private DVD in his head. Just completely zoned out.

"Shall we order you something else?" Avery's dad asked the stepmother. Avery wasn't the biggest fan of her stepmother, and most of the time didn't even call her by name. She assumed—or hoped—that the stepmother wouldn't be around long enough to actually need a name. Although she'd been around for almost a year now. "You know chocolate can trigger your migraines, Elise."

The stepmother smiled at him. "I know, but I love it. So I'll risk a little piece." She smiled at Avery. "Chocolate is worth it, am I right?"

Whatever. Avery didn't bother answering. She took a bite of her cake and hoped everybody would hurry up and finish eating. She wanted to know all the deets about her room renovation and see whatever else she was getting. There was a stack of wrapped gifts on the extra chair. How did you wrap an extreme room makeover, anyway?

Her dad laughed. "Avery is in the present zone, honey," he told the stepmother. "You'll get to the point where you recognize it. The eyes darting to the packages, the lack of patience for anything that gets in the way of opening presents, the hands making involuntary paper ripping motions."

"They do not," Avery muttered, suddenly feeling like a five-year-old.

"I love presents, too," the stepmother said.

She was always doing that—pointing out things she and Avery had in common. It was kind of sad how she kept trying to be Avery's BFF. Although, join the club. Most of the girls at Avery's school acted the same way. It looked kind of pathetic on them, too.

They all needed to grow some self-esteem and not try so hard.

Avery took another bite of cake. The frosting was almost as dense as fudge. Now that she thought about it, she would be willing to take some risks for chocolate, at least chocolate this good. And it wasn't like she was *never* going to be able to open her gifts.

In fact, about twelve minutes later, she had the first one in her hands. She ripped it open. She couldn't help it. She'd always been a ripper. "This is so cool! Thanks!" She ran her fingers over a belt buckle with her initials on it. There was also a buckle in the shape of a Celtic knot and one in the shape of a snowflake, and three straps the buckles could go with. A bronze one, a pink one, and a black one.

"Elise picked those out," her dad told her.

"Thanks," she said again, glancing briefly at Elise. The stepmother. She was actually better at picking out fashion-type presents than Avery's own mother was. And her father—he wasn't allowed to pick out anything Avery (or anyone else, for that matter) would be wearing. Not after the jumpsuit incident three years ago. Yellow. Cotton. Baggy.

Avery pretended to be interested when Peter went all ecstatic over a bunch of movies she'd never heard of. "This is exactly what I need. Early Brando, Nicholson, Newman. It's perfect!" he exclaimed.

Then it was Avery's turn again. Some bath bombs. Nice. She could always use some bath bombs. But it was that last box she *really* needed to open. She had to wait while Peter unwrapped another gift. Some book.

It was finally her turn again. The last box was pretty big. Maybe it had all the paint chips and carpet samples she'd seen in her dad's briefcase inside? It seemed too big for that. And when her father handed it too her, it felt too heavy. Maybe it was some kind of trick. Like there was a decorating magazine and a brick inside. Her dad had that kind of cornball sense of humor sometimes.

Avery tore open the paper and jerked off the lid of the box, then whipped off the layer of tissue paper blocking her view. There was a pair of tall, black riding boots nestled inside. Riding boots?!

"Those come with riding lessons," her father told her.

Avery nodded and forced a smile. "I've been wanting lessons," she said.

"I know. That's why Elise and I got them for you," he answered. "We decided it would be better than getting you something you *didn't* want."

What about all the hints? Avery thought as Peter started tearing into his last present. She'd dropped so many hints. If hints were rocks, her father would be dead by now. It was like he hadn't listened to a word she'd said since she came back from camp. Riding was something she'd been talking about in the spring. Was that the last time he'd actually been paying any attention to her?

"Happy birthday again, you two!" her father exclaimed.

"Yes, happy birthday!" Elise chimed in.

Peter had already finished unwrapping his gift

and Avery hadn't even noticed what it was. Not that she cared. She just wanted to get home to her un-extreme-makeovered bedroom where she wouldn't have to pretend that her birthday had been perfect.

But Avery's father interrupted her gloomy thoughts. "Before we go, Elise and I have some great news, and we thought this would be the perfect time to tell you," he said. "Because it's news about a birthday . . ." He looked over at Elise and smiled, and in the candlelight it looked like his eyes were damp. "In about six months, our family is going to have another birthday to celebrate."

Avery's stomach tightened into a fist. Suddenly everything started to make perfect sense. The paint chips, the swatches, Elise's weight . . . *Don't say it*, she thought. *Please don't say it.*

"Peter, Avery, you're going to have a new baby brother or sister. Elise is pregnant!" Her dad took the stepmother's hand and gave it a squeeze.

So that was it. That was why her dad hadn't picked up on any of her hints. That's why he hadn't been paying any attention to her. For the last three months, all he'd been able to think about was his precious new baby. Forget about his old kids.

She looked over at Peter, expecting to see some of her horror reflected in his eyes. But he just said "congratulations" and started reading the back of one of his new DVDs.

"Congratulations," Avery forced herself to echo. "That's great news."

For you two, she silently added. *I may as well run away and join the circus. It's not like any of you*—she shot a disgusted look at her brother, who should be sharing the tragedy with her—*would notice.*

chapter
SIX

After social studies, Natalie headed directly to the closest girl's room. She moved as quickly as possible without breaking into a run or doing some kind of dorky speed walk. It was Wednesday, her third day of school as a person of the orthodontured persuasion, and she'd already developed a system.

Social studies was her last class before lunch. That's why she went directly to the bathroom. She locked herself in the stall closest to the door, because she'd noticed that people always went for the stalls farthest from the door first. After locking herself in, she waited until she figured that pretty much everyone with her lunch period had made it to the cafeteria. That's when she made her move to the library—when no one would stop her and ask why she wasn't heading to the caf.

Once she was inside the library, she grabbed *The History of Western Art*—the largest book she'd been able to find—propped it open in front of herself at the back table farthest from the windows, and covertly ate her lunch behind it. There were rules against eating in the library, so Natalie had started to bring noncrunchy food. Not that she could eat yummy crunchy food with those horrible metal bars on her teeth, anyway.

Yeah, I've got this down, Natalie thought as she slipped into the first stall before anyone else had reached the bathroom. She refused to let herself think about how many months she'd have to quarantine herself during lunch. If she went there, she might sink down on the floor and curl up in a ball and cry. They'd have to call the janitor to come and get her out.

Natalie heard footsteps come into the bathroom and stop in front of the sinks. She estimated that approximately three-fifths of the girls at her school did some kind of makeup and/or hair repair before hitting the lunchroom.

"Do you *really* believe that Ms. Grandin isn't going to read our journal entries?" Natalie heard a familiar voice ask. It was Hannah, her best noncamp friend. "I know she said she wouldn't. But when she's flipping through to see if we wrote our pages, don't you think she might read some, even kind of accidentally?"

"What did you write? It sounds juicy!" another voice teased. Natalie thought it was Jayne Coben, but she wasn't positive. She was definitely sure about the Hannah ID, though. She'd logged way too many hours of phone time with Hannah not to know her voice.

Hannah giggled. "A little juicy." She sounded a little embarrassed, and Natalie could so picture the expression on her friend's face. What was this juiciness? And why hadn't she told Nat?

Oh, right. Because Hannah had treated her the same way Colette had. She'd acted all uncomfortable and awkward with the new, braces on, freaky Natalie.

"Tell me," Probably Jayne urged.

"No way. And as long as Ms. Grandin keeps her promise, no one's ever going to know," Hannah answered.

"Natalie could get it out of you," Probably Jayne said.

True. Natalie smiled. But the smile faded almost right away. *Was it still true?* she wondered. Getting Hannah's secrets out was a friend thing. It didn't feel like they were even friends anymore.

"Or is that even true now?" Probably Jayne asked. "Natalie's so weird lately."

She's going to defend me, Natalie told herself. Maybe they weren't exactly friends anymore. They didn't even eat lunch together. But they *had* been friends practically forever. Hannah would come up with something nice to say about her.

"I know," Hannah finally said. "She's a completely different person than she was last week. It's . . . I can't even describe it."

Last week. As in when she didn't have braces. Hot tears stung Natalie's eyes. She blinked hard until they disappeared.

Hannah and Probably Jayne moved on to the subject of Kenyon Smith, and about thirty seconds later they were gone. It took about ten minutes for the whole bathroom to clear out, then Natalie proceeded to the library. She had a routine, and she was going to stick to it. It was working for her.

Barely. But working.

▲ ▲ ▲

Natalie closed the door of the apartment she shared with her mother behind her, then let out a long breath. Muscles in her shoulders that she hadn't realized were tight relaxed. She was home. She didn't need a routine here. She didn't have to remember to try to talk with her mouth mostly closed. She didn't have to remember not to smile.

She was alone a lot—like now. And when her mom was home, well, she treated Natalie like Natalie. Braces or no braces.

Not like Hannah.

Natalie didn't want to think about her. She'd do her homework later, but that was the only thought she wanted to put into anything school-related. She got out her ruby red laptop, curled up on the sofa, and checked out the camp blog. She hadn't read it since she got her braces, and it always gave her an almost-back-at-camp feeling.

Bring me the happy, she thought as she started to read.

Posted by: Jenna
Subject: McMoldy??

Confess, Sarah. Did you see Sam Quinn before he got his makeup on? How much work has he had done?

He wears a toupee, doesn't he? Aren't you now totally embarrassed you found him crushable?

Posted by: Brynn
Subject: I'm in love

I know you all thought I was in love with acting before. *I* thought I was in love with acting before. But being a professional actor—because being an extra is a professional gig—it's phenomenal. To be part of a group of people all working together on one project, it's like being a bee in this really groovy hive. (Sorry, I've been a '70s girl named Dawn all weekend.) It's amazing how many people it takes to make a movie. I'm never walking out before the credits are done again. Usually, I leave after the actors go by, but not now.

Thanks for being the Hollywood connection, Nat. You in for next weekend? They're shooting a sock hop scene. Fun, no? And they'll need a ton of extras. Come! Please! I'll be your best friend! And I need one since Sarah can't stop looking at a certain guy. It's not Sam Quinn, but that's all I'm sayin'. You'll have to ask her for the scoopage.

I'm off to practice my bop.

There were a lot more posts, but Natalie suddenly didn't feel like reading them. Brynn's had sent her thoughts spiraling to a bad place. Like would Brynn really be her friend if Natalie showed up on set with her booby-trapped face? Or would she be like Hannah and start bad-mouthing Natalie behind her back?

Plus there was Sarah and this mystery guy, who Brynn had called cute when she and Natalie talked on the phone on Saturday. Natalie was happy that Sarah seemed to be falling in like with a cute boy. She was. But she didn't really want to witness it up close. Not when there was no potential that she was going have anybody in like with her for a long time.

Well, except for Eli, who had been really happy when she'd gone over and talked to him in the park. He didn't care about her braces, because he had braces himself. Wait a second. Hadn't Natalie read something about two teens kissing and getting their braces locked together and having to go to the emergency room?

Didn't matter. She and Eli weren't anywhere near the kissing stage, and she didn't see them getting there. He was just someone to hang with—a boy to hang with—who didn't have a pre-braces Natalie in his head to compare the current Natalie with. True, he was a scooch boring. But you couldn't have everything. Especially not when even one of your best friends thought you were weird.

Natalie pulled the scrap of paper with Eli's e-mail on it out of her backpack. A little e-chat with him might cheer her up. She added him to her buddy list and—voila!—he was online.

<NatalieNYC>: so what is luff again?

Eli shot her a smiling, green head holding a sign that said "LOL."

\<ModelGuy\>: Nat! Hi! Luff is getting close enough to the wind that the sail flaps. It's also what you call the forward edge of a sail. The outside edge of the sail is called the leech.

\<NatalieNYC\>: u know ur stuff.

"And you like to talk about it a lot," she murmured to herself. Eli answered with one of those blushing face emoticons.

\<ModelGuy\>: It took me a long time. I actually made flash cards.

He added a head-scratching emoticon. Natalie was getting the feeling that anything Eli liked, he liked a lot.

\<ModelGuy\>: So what's up? What have you been doing?

An emoticon of a smiling, chin-scratching face appeared. Natalie rolled her eyes and smiled, but didn't send Eli an eye-rolling emoticon. Or a smiley one. She didn't want to encourage him.

She thought for a moment. What was she supposed to tell him about what she'd been doing, anyway? That she'd been spending a lot of time in the first stall of the second floor girl's bathroom?

Natalie restlessly flicked her fingers across the keyboard, then answered Eli's question.

<NatalieNYC>: i've gotten kinda into art lately.

She *had* spent days behind *The History of Western Art*.

<ModelGuy>: Cool. All I know about art is the painting I do for my models.

He sent her a winking dog. Cute. But . . . why? Natalie guessed cuteness was enough of a reason.

Before she could decide on what to say next, another message from Eli popped up.

<ModelGuy>: I'm also into model trains. There's a convention on Sunday at the Javits Center. Wanna go with me? You'd be able to run some of the trains, and trains are easier to control than sailboats. No wind factor.

Natalie waited for the emoticon. She got a sound instead. A long train whistle.

Hmm. A model train convention. That didn't exactly spell F.U.N. But by the weekend, Nat knew she'd be in the extreme lonely zone, and she already knew she didn't want to be an extra at the sock hop. Well, she did. But only if they turned the film into a horror movie and needed all the extras to wear masks.

<NatalieNYC>: i'm there. sounds fun.

⛺ ⛺ ⛺

Avery heard the blender purring. She and Peter were the only ones home that afternoon. Perfect. She'd been wanting to talk to him for days, ever since The Announcement on Sunday.

"What are we going to do?" she asked as she stepped through the kitchen doorway.

"About what?" Peter poured himself a glass of thick, greenish pink liquid from the blender.

Avery couldn't believe her brother's response. "We established a long time ago that I'm the more intelligent—and better looking—twin," Avery teased. "But how can you ask 'about what'? Have you not even thought about the baby situation in the past three days?"

"Doesn't matter to me, as long as they don't expect me to babysit," Peter answered. He started toward his room, leaving the gunk-filled blender on the counter.

Avery followed him. "Don't think you're going to get away with being a slob like that after the baby's born. The stepmother's not going to have time to clean up after you. You'll be getting lectures on how you're way past old enough to take care of yourself."

Peter shrugged.

"And there will be crying," Avery continued. "Both of our rooms are close to the guest room. Don't think you'll be able to sleep through the howling and wailing. Plus the smell of baby poo will probably fill up the whole house."

"I guess we'll have to stock up on air freshener and earplugs," Peter said in a slightly mocking tone. "It's not going to be that bad, Ave."

Her brother just wasn't getting it. "Look, I've been thinking about it, and I figured out Dad stopped listening to me right about when the stepmother found out she was pregnant." Peter went into his room and tried to shut the door behind him. Avery blocked it with her foot. "You might not care now, but you're going to care when there's something you really want and you can't get Dad's attention for even three seconds," she warned him.

Peter flopped down on his bed and clicked the television remote. An old movie popped up on the screen. "I want to study this."

She was trying to talk to him about his life and he wanted to watch a movie in black-and-white. Hello. Color? High def? "You know what you're like? You're like someone who's told a hurricane is coming right toward his house and refuses to evacuate."

Peter clicked the remote again, turning the volume up. At least he was watching a talkie. Sometimes he even watched the silent ones.

"Don't come crying to me when you're sitting in a tree with water up to your butt," Avery tried again.

Peter didn't answer.

There was no one she could talk to in this house. No one!

chapter
SEVEN

"Lowell, hi! Aren't you going the wrong way?" Brynn called as she spotted her fellow castmate walking toward the train station on Saturday. Brynn was walking the opposite direction, away from the station, toward the movie set.

"They decided to shoot a different scene today," Lowell said, stopping in front of her. "They don't need any kid extras at all."

"No way!"

Lowell nodded his head. "Tell me about it. I had to get up at 4:30 to get here on time," Lowell told her. "But we're on for tomorrow at 3:00. So, you heading back to the station?"

"I want to try and find Sarah," Brynn answered. That way she could still salvage some fun out of the day. And she wasn't quite ready for another couple hours on the train.

"I didn't see her. Chace was at the bus stop, though. He's the one who gave me the head's up. He might still be there if his bus hasn't come," Lowell said. "I guess I'll see you tomorrow." He gave a half salute as he started toward the train station again.

"Bye!" Brynn called over her shoulder. She hurried toward the set in the hopes of catching Sarah. Along the way, she passed the bus stop where she thought she might find Chace. He was a Connecticut boy, so he could ride the bus to the set instead of taking the train, but there was no sign of him. She was surprised he hadn't decided to stay and find Sarah, too.

A block later, she reached the college. As she cut across the green lawn, heading toward the gym/wardrobe room—that's where Sarah would go first—Brynn spotted Temple, the girl with the long pony-tails from last weekend. Temple waved, and Brynn waved back.

A few seconds later, she had one of those delayed realizations, the kind where her eyes processed info a little faster than her brain. She'd seen Temple in her '70s outfit, but it hadn't sunk in immediately that Temple was in *costume*. Ready to shoot a scene. Although obviously not the '50s sock hop scene.

Brynn looked around for a PA. They were easy to recognize. Half the time they looked like they were talking to themselves as they relayed information through the small headsets they all wore. *There's one,* she thought, picking out a guy who looked like he could also be a student at the college where the movie was being filmed. When she got closer, she confirmed that, yup, he had on a headset.

"Um, excuse me," she said. "Are you using the kid extras today?" She felt a little silly asking the question. There were kid extras around everywhere. She didn't see anyone leaving.

"We're reshooting the hallway scene we did on Saturday. Zan wasn't happy with the lighting. So if you were in the scene then, you're in it now," the PA answered.

That scene took place in the '70s, which meant Brynn would be Dawn again. As she got in line for wardrobe, she tried to get back in Dawn's head. Dawn had an oral report to give. So Brynn figured she might be feeling a little—

"No spilling!"

The shout pulled Brynn away from her thoughts. She turned toward the sound and saw Chace poking Sarah and pretending to get her to spill her hot coffee.

"I thought you went home," Brynn called out to Chace.

"What?" Sarah asked. She took a tiny sip of her coffee.

"No talking! Now is the time we dance!" Chace handed Brynn a mochachino, then used his free hand to spin her around, bringing her into the dance.

"Are you always going to be saving a place for them?" someone waiting behind Brynn in the costume line complained.

Chace pointed at the complainer. "Somebody needs to be dancing."

And, to Brynn's surprise, the somebody actually

smiled and started to dance. She didn't know how serious Chace was about acting, but she bet he'd be good at it. Maybe not the tapping into emotions part. But he definitely had the glow, the *it factor*. People responded to him, liked him.

"Hey, I spotted a movie theater a couple blocks from here," Chace said. "We should go see something sometime. Check out the stylings of the extras."

"Really, Lowell said he saw you at the bus stop," Brynn tried again.

Chace stopped dancing. "Yeah, I got here and a PA told me there was a schedule change and they didn't need any kid extras, so I left. I saw Lowell on his way here and explained the dealio. Then I realized I'd left my backpack by the fountain. I came back over and saw people in their '70s costumes and found out the PA had gotten it wrong. There was a schedule change, but only to reshoot the hallway scene."

Huh. Brynn guessed that Chace's explanation could be true. But all the PAs seemed incredibly organized. It was a little hard to believe one of them could make such a big mistake. Was Chace lying again?

She still hadn't decided a couple hours later when she, Chace, and Sarah were in their places in the hallway. Brynn stood in front of her locker, hairbrush in hand.

"Background!" the AD called.

Brynn began brushing her hair, thinking of her oral report. Footsteps pounded down the hall. Sam Quinn began to shout. She turned toward him. It's true what they say about acting being all about reacting. When you hear somebody yell in a panic, you look. It's natural.

Sam leaped over Chace, who was kneeling in the middle of the hall, tying his shoe. "Smooth move, Six Million Dollar Man," he called after Sam.

After Zan called "cut," Brynn's brain played catch-up again. *Chace* had done the "smooth move" line. She'd seen and heard him, but she hadn't taken the next step and thought—Chace is doing Lowell's line. Chace had told Lowell to leave this morning. Had—

"Where's my redhead?" Zan asked the AD. Brynn turned her attention to them. She was very curious to hear how it would go down.

"Chace told me he wasn't here, so I threw Chace in instead," the AD answered.

Brynn's stomach did a slow roll. Chace had told Lowell the schedule had changed *and* he had also told the AD Lowell wasn't on the set that day.

Zan nodded. "Good job," she told Chace.

And that's a SAG voucher for Chace! Brynn thought.

Chace grinned, and Brynn suddenly remembered his reaction when Lowell got the line the last time they shot this scene. Chace's happiness for Lowell had seemed a little forced.

Brynn got the same feeling she did when she drank a milkshake too fast. Cold gut. Sharp pain in the head.

Could Chace have told Lowell to go home so Chace could get the line? That meant Chace's whole story about the PA's mistake was definitely a lie.

But Brynn had seen Chace lie before. He was good at it.

▲ ▲ ▲

This many people care about little trains? Natalie wondered Sunday morning as she climbed the wide stairs crowded with people up to the Javits Center. Her cell beeped just as she was starting to look around for Eli.

Sarah had sent her a pic. It showed her wearing jeans tucked into slouchy boots and a green cowl-neck sweater. A second later a text from Sarah arrived.

Do I look okay? I have a date. And he only asked me last night, so I've only been able to try on everything in my closet twelve or thirteen times.

I barely thought about what I put on today, Natalie realized as she began texting Sarah back.

you look smashing, stunning, stupefying. i've run out of s words. gotta go. i see my own date.

Natalie snapped her phone shut. Walking toward her was Eli, wearing a bright orange T-shirt that said: "Still Plays With Trains."

"I wore orange so I'd be easier to spot," he told her. "But I've already seen at least twenty other people in this shirt."

"Well, I found you," Natalie answered. *With your freckle accessories and your adorable shaggy hair.* He really *was* cute.

Eli smiled at her and, for the first time, Natalie realized his braces alternated between red and blue, tooth by tooth. She'd avoided looking at his mouth, the way she hoped he—and everyone—would avoid looking at hers.

Eli noticed the direction of her gaze. "Giants fan," he explained.

He'd done something to draw attention to his teeth. "Cool," Natalie told him. And it was. Sort of. Eli showed no fear and *that* was cool, even if a red and blue grill—not so much.

"You ready to go in?" Eli asked. "I already got tickets."

"Let's do this thing," Natalie answered. She felt her eyes widen as they entered the main area of the convention center. There were hundreds of displays. Maybe even a thousand. The sound of a multitude of engines and wheels on tracks could be heard under the music.

"Thomas the Train is here," Natalie said.

"Yeah, the NMRA—National Model Railroad Association—wants to get more kids interested in the hobby. And also have something fun for little kids to do. We have to check out the Lego train. They always come up with something awesome, all made out of Legos. But first, I wanted to stop by the booth of one of the local clubs. Some of my friends are in it.

Is that okay?"

"This is a strange, new world for me. You're the guide," Natalie told him. "So why aren't you in the club?" she asked as they snaked their way through the crowd, past a demonstration of wiring techniques, a booth with a huge number of miniature plants for sale, and a nacho stand.

"I had to choose between the regatta at the pond or the club. I didn't have time for both," Eli explained. "There they are. E-11." He led Natalie over to a table with a model train—of course—on it. Four guys and a girl wearing matching "I've Been Working on the Railroad" hoodies stood at the booth. They were clearly the club members. Natalie could tell by their mix of pride and concern as they watched the train run over the tracks.

"Lookin' good," Eli told the closest guy.

"We were still working on it five minutes before the doors opened," the guy confessed.

"Nat, this is Clive." A girl wandered over to join them. "And that's Rachel."

"So what was the problem?" Eli asked. "Clive was telling me you were scrambling to get running."

"We had a derailment issue," Rachel said. She ran her fingers through her thick, black hair. Natalie liked the asymmetrical cut.

"Let me guess." Eli closed his eyes for a minute in thought. "Coupler problem with your Hi Cube Boxcar."

"Not even close," Rachel said. "Switch problem. There was a rail joiner that wasn't connected correctly.

I found it with a curve gauge." Her big, gray eyes sparkled with pleasure as she slapped Eli a high five.

"Rachel and I live across the street from each other," Eli told Natalie. "We've been into trains since Rachel's mom bought one to go around the Christmas tree when we were, like, seven."

"We tried to make improvements right away," Rachel said.

"And started a small fire," Eli added.

"You can still see the singe marks on the bottom of our artificial tree." Rachel smiled. "So how do you two know each other? I thought I knew everybody Eli knew."

"Not quite," Eli said. "We met at the pond."

"Oh, you're one of the model *boat* people." Rachel shook her head. "You guys don't even get to make buildings or do landscape. It's just your boat."

"Yesterday was actually the first time I worked a model boat," Natalie admitted. "Eli showed me how."

"Huh," Rachel said, looking back and forth between Eli and Natalie. "So what are you into?"

What was she into? Fashion. Camp, but not the really outdoorsy parts of camp. Magazine quizzes and beauty tips. She was into hanging out with her friends, back when she had some. She liked sushi. But it's not like she could give that as a major interest.

"Natalie's into art," Eli finally answered for her.

That was sort of true. Besides spending time with *The History of Western Art*, Natalie's mom was an art dealer, so Nat had gone to a lot of art galleries. Some she loved, some were fascinating in a freaky way, some did nothing for her, and some just made her want to leave.

"Have you ever worked with Polly S or MRC/Tamiya?" Clive asked.

Natalie sucked in a breath, then admitted, "I don't even know what they are."

"They're flat water-based acrylics," Eli explained. "They don't have solvents that attack the plastic or paint of the models."

"I used Polly S to do the weathering on the water tower. Now, I'm wondering if I should have gone that way at all. Maybe I should have used chalk dust," Clive said.

That launched a whole conversation filled with many terms Natalie had never heard of before. She tried to stay engaged in the conversation, but it was like Clive, Eli, and Rachel were speaking another language. Eli kept translating, but even the translation was confusing.

And, even though she didn't want to admit it, the whole thing was boring. Not to them, obviously. But she was almost bored out of her mind.

Suck it up, she told herself. *Eli's nice. He is. And cute. And he doesn't care about your braces at all. And it's better to be bored than boyless.*

chapter
EIGHT

Avery rolled over and checked her alarm clock. 10:30. She supposed she should head down to the kitchen. Sunday morning brunch was the one meal her father cooked, and it was ridiculous—pancakes with chocolate chips, eggs, bacon and sausage, bagels, three kinds of cream cheese, lox, biscuits. Sometimes he even went out to Krispy Kreme for warm donuts. Complete ridiculousness.

He and the stepmother—and usually Peter and Avery—didn't get dressed until afternoon. Sometimes her dad didn't get dressed the entire day. He sat around the table reading the paper. Make that papers. He liked the *New York Times*, but he hated how it didn't have the funnies, so he got the local paper, too. He'd read everyone their horoscope out loud, making half of it up, and then he'd read the cartoons with these stupid voices. Avery tried to have friends sleep over on Friday nights, never Saturdays. Sunday mornings with her father were just a little too . . . ridiculous.

Avery padded downstairs in her Sunday-morning-only slippers. She'd had them for years. They were shaped like cows and had little bells on them. The bottoms were almost worn through.

"What's going on?" she asked as she stepped through the kitchen door.

"Your father's been reading." The stepmother nodded toward a stack of books on the table where the papers were usually spread out. Avery scanned the titles: *What to Expect When You're Expecting. The Mayo Guide to a Healthy Pregnancy. A Child is Born. The Expectant Father. The Belly Book. Eating for Pregnancy. What to Expect When Your Wife Is Expecting.*

"We went to the bookstore yesterday, and he went a little crazy," the stepmother added.

"We need every one of those," Avery's father said. He was chopping bits of apple. Avery figured they were going into the vat of oatmeal on the stove. Oatmeal. The only sign of breakfast. Not that she usually ate all—or most—of the food her dad dished up on Sundays. But it was fun to have the huge selection.

"But you already have two kids," Avery answered. "You were around when Mom was pregnant with us, right?" She heard her voice crack a little, and she hated it.

"I know. That's what I said. I told him nothing much about pregnancy has changed since then." The stepmother laughed. "He bought a whole stack of books on being a father, too. As if he isn't already an amazing father. Am I right?"

He used to be, Avery thought. *He used to always get my hints. And if my voice did that babyish cracking thing, he used to always notice.* "Sure, whatever," she said aloud.

"How's that for an endorsement?" Avery's father asked the stepmother. He set a bowl of oatmeal topped with apple bits and walnuts in front of her, giving her pregnant stomach an affectionate pat.

"From a teenager, that's the highest praise you're going to get," the stepmother told him.

"Want a bowl, Ave?" her dad asked. He ladled her some oatmeal before she could answer. When he handed her the bowl, Avery obediently sat down, even though she wasn't sure she wanted to be there.

He grabbed a bowl for himself and sat down, too, then pulled a book from the pile and started reading to himself. No horoscopes? No funnies in his dumb voices? Avery never thought she'd miss them. But she did.

"Avery, you have awesome taste," the stepmother said.

Yeah, and, Avery thought.

"I was wondering if you might like to help me decorate the nursery," she continued.

"Great idea!" Avery's dad chimed in.

The oatmeal, sweet with apples and brown sugar, suddenly tasted sour in Avery's mouth. She forced herself to swallow it. This was unbelievable. Her father thought it was a *great idea* for her to decorate the new little ankle-biter's room? While her own room stayed a disgusting pit?

"I'm going to be pretty busy," Avery muttered,

not speaking directly to either the stepmother or her father. "This semester is really intense. Big paper for English. Team project in science. Maybe you should hire someone."

She stood up and grabbed her bowl. "Actually, I think I'll finish eating in my room. I can do some research on the computer at the same time." She bolted before they could say anything.

▲ ▲ ▲

Sarah's mom had a pair of sneakers with springs in the soles, and Sarah felt like she was wearing them. Each step she took felt light and bouncy. She was *actually* going on a date with Chace! He hadn't called it a date, but the two of them were going to the movies together before they had to be on the set that afternoon, *just* the two of them, not as part of a group, which to Sarah equaled date. How great was it that they didn't have to be getting ready for wardrobe until three this Sunday? That gave her hours of alone time with Chace.

When she turned the corner, she saw him waiting for her in front of the theater near the college campus and the nonexistent springs in her shoes got more springy. Or else gravity wasn't working as well. Now with each step Sarah felt like she might just bounce up, up, up and never come down.

"Hi," she said when she reached him. Her voice came out light and breathy. No other guy made her feel the way Chace did. Happy—springy, bouncy, flying-happy—but kind of nervous at the same time.

He was just so . . . Sarah couldn't think of exactly what word described him. Maybe there wasn't one word. It was like Chace was a lightbulb and everyone else were moths. Her English teacher wouldn't like that analogy. She'd say it was cliché. But Chace drew people to him. And somehow Sarah drew him back. She was the moth the lightbulb flew toward. Except lightbulbs were stationary, so that analogy really didn't work.

Anyway, it made her feel a little nervous being the special moth. It was hard not to wonder why the lightbulb picked her.

Danger Girl is supposed to have a lot of crowd scenes. It should be great for extra evaluating," Chace said.

"Great." Not that Sarah really cared too much about being the best extra in the movie. She wanted to do a good job, but she didn't see this as the beginning of a career the way Brynn and Chace did. She just thought it would be fun.

And it definitely was. Her favorite part was all the waiting, because that's when she could just hang with Chace and Brynn and all the new kids she'd met. Chace always came up with something cool for them to do during the downtime. He'd even gotten a couple of the real actors involved in a game of charades yesterday. Sam Quinn had actually joined in for a round. She had *actually* been playing charades with Sam Quinn because Chace had called him over and invited him. Just like that.

Chace opened the theater door for her and

ushered her inside. Sarah took a deep breath. She loved the smell of greasy movie theater popcorn mixed with that bright yellow nacho gloop.

"I'm starved. I have to get some snacks," Chace announced, walking directly to the concession stand.

"Definitely," Sarah agreed.

"Want to share a popcorn?"

She *so* did. Sharing a popcorn was one step away from holding hands, with all that finger contact as you both reached into the bucket at the same time. Was that why he'd suggested it?

"Sure," Sarah said, trying to play it cool.

"I have to warn you, though, I like to do something strange with my popcorn," Chace told her.

Sarah raised her eyebrows. "Strange?" she repeated. How strange could you get with popcorn?

"I like to mix Dots in it," he said.

Dots. As in that candy that was always so stale it almost made your teeth crack. Then when you did finally manage to chew it, it was so sticky it almost glued your teeth together.

"If you think that's gross—I know a lot of people do—we could ask for one of those cardboard trays and divide the popcorn up," Chace suggested.

"No," Sarah said quickly. "I've never tried popcorn that way, but it sounds good." Lie. But it did sound worth the price to have the sort-of hand-holding with Chace.

Chace ordered, and before she could stop him, he ordered two macchiatos to wash down the Dots-and-popcorn combo. *That's what I get,* Sarah thought. *I keep drinking them every day on set and pretending they're yummy.*

Now she'd probably have Dots ruining her perfectly good greasy popcorn for the rest of her life. Although maybe that wouldn't be so bad if they came with Chace. Even with the caramel macchiato thrown in.

It definitely wouldn't be so bad, she decided as they sat in the theater, waiting for the previews to start. Chace noticed the charm bracelet Sarah was wearing, the one she'd had since she was nine, and asked her to explain the meaning behind every single charm—the bat from her visit to Carlsbad Caverns, the baseball because of the Sox, the teeny copy of *Little Women*, all of them. He wouldn't let her skip one.

Chace cared about her in a way no other guy ever had. He was interested in everything about her. Ev-er-y-thing. She really liked that.

She also liked the way his warm fingers felt against hers as they shared the disgusting mix of popcorn and Dots. And when the popcorn and Dots were gone, she loved the way it felt when he twined his fingers together with hers and didn't let go for the rest of the movie.

chapter
NINE

Brynn sat on the edge of the fountain in the college quad, scanning the movie section of a paper she'd borrowed from one of the PAs.

Several drops of water splashed onto the page. Raining? It had been sunny—

No, not raining, Brynn realized. Chace had flicked some water at her. He and Sarah were standing next to her, smiling.

"Great, you're here." Brynn stood up. "The schedule was changed again today. They still need us, but not for two hours. We can just make it to the next showing of *Danger Girl* if we leave right now. It's playing at the theater a couple blocks away. Remember how you were saying we should check out the technique of some extras?" she asked Chace.

"Hey, PA Dude," Chace called to a guy standing a few feet away wearing a headset.

"Hey, Smooth Move Dude," the PA called back.

"What's the latest on the schedule?" Chace asked.

"We don't need you guys here until five for wardrobe!" He waved and headed toward the coffee tent.

Didn't he trust me? The thought slithered through Brynn's mind. *Is that because he lied to Lowell about the schedule change yesterday, so he suspects everyone else of lying as well?*

Brynn tried to exterminate the thought. She had no proof against Chace. Things could have gone down exactly the way he said they had, with a PA making a mistake and Chace finding out the correct information when he came back to the set for his backpack. And Chace could have told the AD just because it was definitely something the AD needed to know. And the AD could have decided to put Chace in the scene just because Chace was handy. Everything could have happened exactly the way Chace said it had.

Her stomach twisted itself into a knot of protest. Brynn ignored it. "So, what do you say?" she asked Sarah and Chace. "The movie lets out at 4:50. If we hurry, we can make it back here right on time."

Sarah and Chace exchanged a glance. One of those glances that contains a whole private conversation.

"Problem?" Brynn asked.

"Um, Brynn, Chace and I just went to see *Danger Girl*. We came here right from the theater," Sarah admitted.

Oh, so that's what the eye conversation was

about. Brynn thought all three of them had talked about going to a movie together. Somehow three had ended up as two, without Brynn in the loop.

Sarah grabbed the paper. "Maybe there's something else we can all go see now. I'm totally up for a double feature."

"I checked before, and that's the only theater close enough to walk to," Chace said. "And it's old-school—one movie only, not a multiplex. But you should go, Brynn. You'd really like it. There was this one scene where—No, I'm not even going to tell you. It would spoil it. Sarah and I will grab a slice of pizza or something, and then we can all meet up back here."

Where you'll expect me to be holding your places in the wardrobe line as usual, Brynn thought. She looked at Sarah, wondering if her friend would suggest Brynn forget about the movie and come to lunch with them instead.

"It was a really great movie, Brynn," Sarah told her. "And there were lots of crowd scenes, so there's good extra-watching, too."

So that was how it was. "Okay, I guess I'll go. To the movies. By myself." Brynn didn't bother saying good-bye, just turned and walked away fast. She needed to *move*. She couldn't stand to be with them another second. Although she wondered if they'd even notice she was gone.

She reached the theater with two minutes to spare, bought her popcorn and soda, and got settled in the mostly empty theater just as the trailers were beginning. She'd gotten her favorite seat—front row center. She loved how the screen dominated her entire field of vision when she sat there. The soundtrack boomed, almost too loud, in her ears. And the movie became her entire world. That's what she needed right now. She needed to be in a completely different world.

But today, when *Danger Girl* started, Brynn had trouble getting into it, even though the movie-watching conditions were perfect. She kept thinking about Sarah and Chace. Where had they been sitting when they watched the movie? Had they been paying attention, or were they so into each other, they didn't even care what was on the screen? Had Sarah even remembered that the three of them had thought about hitting a movie together?

Watch the movie, she told herself. She returned her attention to the screen, but she was confused. Was the guy with the beard following Danger Girl the smooth-shaven guy from Danger Girl's agency? He sort of looked the same. Was that guy a double agent? *Somebody* was definitely a double agent. Was Danger Girl a double agent?

This was pointless. Brynn did something she'd never done before. She stood up and walked out of the movie. Usually she found bad movies almost as interesting as good ones. She liked to break them down and figure out why they weren't working. She figured it would help her pick scripts in the future, perfect her acting technique, and decide which direc-tors she most wanted to work with. But today her brain was gone. G.O.N.E.

Now what am I going to do? Brynn wondered once she was back out on the sidewalk. She didn't want to accidentally run into Sarah and Chace. She'd feel like a pathetic loser. Even though they were the ones who had acted like jerks.

Brynn decided to call Natalie again. Which was still somewhat pathetic. Natalie had shot her down hard the last time she'd tried to get her to come to the set. And Natalie hadn't answered the post Brynn put on the camp blog telling her that they still needed more extras for the movie.

Still, Brynn was up for giving Natalie another chance. Brynn wouldn't even be an extra if it weren't for Nat. And Natalie had been ultra-supportive of Brynn using the job as an extra to begin her professional career.

She pressed speed dial eight. She could hardly hear Natalie's voice when she said "hello." There was too much background noise.

"Where are you?" Brynn asked, not even bothering to ask her how she was doing or what was up.

"I'm at a model train show," Natalie answered.

"What? I thought I heard you say you were at a model train show. There's a ton of noise on your end," Brynn said.

"I'm moving to a quieter spot. I'm in a corner now. Is that better?" Natalie asked a few seconds later.

"A little. Now, where are you?"

"I told you. A model train show."

"I was sure I heard that wrong. Now my question is—why?" Brynn said.

She definitely heard Natalie's sigh. It was loud and long. "I met this guy who's into model trains."

Was this why Natalie had decided to skip being an extra? A guy?

"The teeny tiny train passengers must dress really well and have some adorable little shoes," Brynn commented. "Or the new boy must be pretty special."

"He is," Natalie said. But she wouldn't get a passing grade in Brynn's drama class with that line delivery.

"What's going on, Nat?"

"Nothing. It's too loud to talk in here, that's all. I'll talk to you later, okay? Bye."

And she was gone.

Don't friends actually tell each other things anymore? Brynn wondered. She gave a sigh as long and loud as Natalie's had been. Then she felt around in the front pockets of her jeans. Good, she still had her ticket stub. She might as well go back inside and try to figure out *Danger Girl*. It would probably be easier than understanding Natalie or Sarah.

▲ ▲ ▲

"Brynn! Brynn!" Sarah called, waving her hands to get her friend's attention.

Brynn slowly—and it seemed to Sarah, very reluctantly—crossed the quad and headed Sarah's way.

"You look amazing. How many petticoats are under there?" Sarah ran her fingers over Brynn's poofy skirt.

Brynn shrugged. "I couldn't save your place in line. You and Chace weren't here, so I went in." Her voice sounded tight.

"Yeah, of course, obviously," Sarah answered. "No worries. Chace is changing. I'll get in line in a minute. Look, Brynn, I just wanted to apologize."

Brynn adjusted the cat's-eye glasses she was wearing as part of her costume. She gave Sarah a go-on look. She was even more upset than Sarah had realized. Not that Sarah blamed her.

"I completely forgot that we talked about going to a movie and watching the extras yesterday. I would have invited you for sure," Sarah said. And she would have. She never would have left Brynn out. That was a complete mean girl move, not something you did to anybody, especially not to a real friend. "Chace texted me last night, and—"

"I guess he forgot, too," Brynn snarked.

"I guess. We only talked about it for a sec. He probably remembered it was something he wanted to do, but didn't remember he'd already mentioned it," Sarah said.

Brynn rolled her eyes.

This *was how she accepted an apology?* Sarah thought. *A completely sincere apology?* "So, do you forgive me?" Sarah barely stopped herself from adding "or what?"

"Yeah."

That was it? Just yeah? Very gracious.

But her apology hadn't been completely sincere, either. Deep—deep, deep, deep—down, Sarah had to admit she was glad she'd forgotten that Chace had brought up going to the movies in front of Brynn. Those two hours sitting in the dark with Chace, holding hands—she wouldn't have wanted to give those up. Not for anything. Not even to protect Brynn's feelings. So she probably didn't deserve a more gracious apology-accepted than she got.

"Hey, babies, are you ready to bop?" Chace asked as he joined them, already in character.

"Wow. Your costume is fabulous. You look like one of the stars of *Grease*," Sarah told him.

Chace stroked the sleeve of his leather jacket. "I sort of do, don't I?" He winked. Sarah so loved his cheesy wink. "I'm just practicing being conceited. It goes with being a greaser."

"None of the guys I saw getting suited up in wardrobe had anything that cool," Brynn said. But it didn't sound like a compliment. It sounded more like an accusation.

"I found it at a Salvation Army store buried under a pile of T-shirts," Chace explained.

Brynn's eyes narrowed behind the cat's-eye glasses. "I need to borrow Sarah for one second," she told Chace.

"Then I have to get to the wardrobe line," Sarah called over her shoulder as Brynn tugged her away.

"What?" Sarah snapped when they were far

enough away from everyone not to be overheard. She pulled her arm away from Brynn's grasp. She was definitely annoyed now.

"I wasn't going to say anything . . . Well, I know I sort of said something the first day, but I wasn't going to say anything else, because I didn't have any proof. But now I have proof," Brynn burst out.

"Take a breath. Slow down. I don't even know what you're talking about," Sarah said.

"Chace. You can't trust him, Sarah. He'll do anything to get noticed on the set, and he doesn't care if he hurts people to do it," Brynn said in a rush.

"Where are you getting this?" Sarah snapped.

"I'm getting it from what he just said, for starters. Extras aren't supposed to do their own costumes on this movie. I'm sure Chace didn't get approval for his outfit. He's just trying to stand out in the crowd," Brynn told her.

"You're the one who showed up with two duffel bags on day one," Sarah reminded her.

"With wigs and glasses. Not costumes. I knew the movie was handling them," Brynn explained.

"What about the other stuff? The tap shoes, and the baseball glove, and the yo-yo, and the sparklers, and the cannon?"

"There was no—"

Sarah didn't let Brynn finish. "The whole point of all that stuff was to get noticed, to get you more screen time, to help you become a star. What's wrong with Chace wanting the same thing?" Brynn was such a hypocrite. Sarah couldn't believe it.

"There's nothing wrong with it if you don't break the rules and hurt people," Brynn shot back.

"Wearing an authentic '50s jacket is going to *hurt* someone?" Sarah demanded. "I think you need a dictionary."

"I wasn't talking about that. I was talking about Lowell." Brynn's face flushed with anger. "Chace stole Lowell's line. And that's more than just a few words. That's a SAG voucher. That's a step toward becoming a professional actor."

"Lowell wasn't here when the scene was reshot. You'd have done the same thing if you'd thought of it first." Sarah's own face felt hot. It was probably as red as Brynn's.

"I wouldn't have cheated Lowell out of it. I wouldn't have purposely lied to him and told him that the extras weren't needed so he wouldn't be around when the scene was reshot," Brynn said. "I wouldn't, and you know that I wouldn't."

"Chace didn't do that, either. You heard him tell us what happened," Sarah argued.

"I heard him lie. I've heard him lie a lot of times," Brynn answered.

Suddenly, Sarah got it. She understood everything. "This is still about me and Chace going to the movie without you. You're feeling left out and jealous and that's why you're saying all this horrible stuff."

Brynn shook her head. "No," she said simply.

"I apologized for leaving you out of the movie," Sarah told Brynn. "And I meant it. If you still want to be my friend, you're going to have to apologize to me for what you said about Chace."

"I'm sorry, but what I said is true, Sarah," Brynn insisted. "And he's probably going to end up hurting you, too. You can't trust him."

Sarah looked at Brynn for a long moment. There had to be something to say, some way to fix this. Her friendship with Brynn couldn't end right here.

But nothing came to Sarah. So she turned around and walked to the wardrobe line. She wrapped her arms tightly around herself. She hated fights. Hated them. But Brynn had been wrong, wrong, wrong.

Sarah avoided Brynn the rest of the day. It wasn't hard. There were a ton of extras, and she made sure she and Chace entered the gym, which had been cleared of wardrobe for the sock hop scene, well after Brynn. The AD ended up placing Sarah and Chace on the opposite side of the room from her, too. Bonus—he assigned Sarah and Chace to be dance partners, and put them in a spot near the actor playing Sam Quinn's son. They'd almost definitely make the final cut.

Had Chace's killer costume had something to do with that? Maybe. Was that wrong—even if it was slightly against the rules? Like Sarah had told Brynn, it didn't hurt anyone, so no.

She didn't believe Brynn's accusations

about Chace sabotaging Lowell. Now that would have been wrong, with a capital W. And a capital R,O,N, and G.

After the last shot, Sarah changed back into her street clothes. Again, that was easy to manage without a Brynn encounter. Lots and lots of girls to use as barricades.

It would be a little harder to avoid Brynn at the train station, but Sarah would do it. She was sure Brynn was avoiding her, too. Which helped.

Anyway, she wasn't going to think about that right now. Right now, she was going to find Chace and enjoy every second of the short walk they'd have together before he had to stop at his bus stop.

Chace came right up to her the second she walked out of the changing room. And as they started across the quad, he grabbed her hand in a no-big-deal way. Sort of like he'd been her boyfriend for months. Did he think of them that way, as a couple?

Sarah gave his hand a slight squeeze, and Chace squeezed her hand back. That seemed couple-ish. She wondered if she should kiss him good-bye on the cheek when they got to the bus stop. She was still considering the pros and cons when they arrived. She decided she would just leave it up to him, she thought as she lingered just a few moments. Or maybe—

"Peter! What are you doing in Guilford?" a guy asked, stepping up next to them and interrupting Sarah's thoughts.

To Sarah's surprise, Chace answered. "I have a

gig as an extra in the new Sam Quinn movie. Sarah, this is Ian. We were on the same tennis team last year."

"Back when Peter's only interest wasn't going Hollywood," Ian said.

"I've heard some weird nicknames, but how do you get Peter from Chace? Or Chace from Peter?" Sarah asked.

"Chace Turner is my screen name. I thought I might as well start using it from the beginning," Chace, or Peter, explained. "My real name is Peter Chace."

"Chace Turner. Good name. I need to get going or I'll miss my train." Sarah tried to walk away in a straight line, even though the sidewalk suddenly felt like it was alive and wriggling around under her feet.

Peter Chace. Who lived in Connecticut. Now Sarah knew exactly where she recognized Chace from. He had almost the exact same face as Avery Chace from Walla Walla. She had always said her twin was really into acting. Peter *had* to be Avery's twin brother. He just had to be.

This was . . . disastrous.

Avery had to have told her brother all about the lonely, pathetic girl who'd told everyone at Walla Walla she was movie-star Tad Maxwell's daughter because she wanted to be popular.

When Peter found out Sarah was that lonely, pathetic girl, she wouldn't be his favorite moth anymore. There was no possible way. Peter could have any girl. A perfect girl. When he found out the truth, he would know Sarah was so *un*perfect. Then he would dump her faster than yesterday's trash. If they were even a couple to begin with.

chapter TEN

Avery wondered if she was hallucinating.

She was sitting in her room after school on Wednesday. Her so-called room. It was so ugly, it should have to have a different name. And she could have sworn she'd heard crying coming from what would be the nursery.

There won't be a squaller in there for months, she told herself. She returned to her algebra homework. Then she heard it again. Softer, but definitely crying.

This is not you, Avery told herself. *You don't have whatever sound hallucinations are called. True, having to deal with Dad and the stepmother's late-in-life baby is not right. But you're not going to have a breakdown. If anything, you're going to give some other people around here breakdowns.*

She looked at the algebra problem again. She liked algebra. It was different than other kinds of math, sliding everything around until you got x on one side. It was sort of like a puzzle. For this one, first she needed to—

There it was again. Avery wasn't crazy. Which meant the sound was real. Which meant somebody was crying in what should still be the guest room. There was nothing to cry about in the guest room.

Avery slammed her math book shut, stood up, and strode out of her room and down the hall to the *guest* room. She was right. The crying was not coming from the spirit of the baby that was going to haunt her for the rest of her life. It was coming from the stepmother. She was sitting on the floor, with her head in her hands, trying—and failing—to get control over herself.

Mystery solved. Avery didn't feel the need to take any action. She'd just do her homework downstairs in the living room.

She slowly began to back up . . . when the stepmother lifted her head. "Oh, Avery, sorry," the stepmother said. "I knew you were home. I guess I didn't know how loud I was."

"Uh, is something wrong?" Avery asked. *Please don't feel the need to share. Or at least phone a friend.*

"I don't know how to decorate the nursery," the stepmother confessed, sniffling.

That was it? There were people who were paid to handle that kind of crisis. Should Avery bring the stepmother the yellow pages or what? "My friend Natalie's mother probably knows some great designers," Avery said, deciding that allowing the stepmother to choose a decorator from the yellow pages was asking for ugly.

The stepmother gave a choked laugh. "No, this is something the mother is supposed to do. It's part of nesting. Instinct. Mother's love. If you don't do the room right, then you'll probably forget to feed the baby and social services will come and take it away."

"My dad makes a good salary, you know. I'm sure you could have a doula. Isn't that what they call a baby nanny?"

The stepmother laughed so hard, Avery thought she might have to slap her to prevent hysteria. "I hadn't even heard that word until after I graduated from college. But then, I didn't grow up in Connecticut."

"You know what they are now, so you could get one." *And stop crying*, Avery added to herself.

"I really want to take care of the baby myself. And decorate the baby's room. It's just—" The stepmother gestured to the baby instruction books scattered all around her on the floor. "They all say something different. And I don't know which one I'm supposed to believe. My sister has kids, and there's my mom, of course, but they're all the way in Ohio. I don't have any family here. And talking on the phone isn't the same, and anyway, they think I'm silly to get so intense about all this and—"

The stepmother was hiccuping now. It sounded like a countdown to more bawling. Avery quickly dropped down onto the floor and picked up the closest book. She did a fast flip-through until a good sentence jumped out at her. "You can do this. It's not that complicated. Listen: 'Babies first respond to primary colors.' So that eliminates a lot of color choices right there."

The stepmother wiped her eyes with her fists,

like a little kid. "But listen to this." She picked up a different book and read a line. "Babies are soothed by pastels." She dropped the book. "I want the baby to be soothed in its nursery, don't I? And then this book . . ." She kicked yet another book across the room. "It says babies see black and white contrast best of all, and that it stimulates their development."

Avery didn't know what to say to that. "I'm starting to understand why you were crying."

The stepmother laughed. But a real laugh this time. Not choking or borderline hysterical.

Avery laughed, too. She couldn't help it.

▲ ▲ ▲

Usually a book could become Sarah's whole world. People could be talking to her when she was reading, and she wouldn't hear them. Her mom always said an entire circus could parade through the room when Sarah had her nose in a book, and Sarah wouldn't notice. Even if the elephant stepped on her foot.

But the usual book magic wasn't working for her today. Every few words, she'd think of Chace. Peter. Had he found out the truth yet? Avery knew that Sarah and Brynn were extras on the movie. She had to know her brother was, too. Eventually, she'd ask if he'd met them. And then she'd tell the *funny* story of how Sarah had pretended she was a movie star's kid to get a little attention at camp.

Had it happened yet? Was it happening right now?

Sarah had asked herself those two questions

about a million times since Sunday. She'd hardly gotten any sleep the last three nights. She'd start to drift off, then the questions would flash through her mind and she'd jerk awake, heart pounding.

"I need help," she muttered, putting her book aside. "I need serious psychological help. Or I need some kind of mind-erase tool that I can use on Chace—and Avery."

Getting psychological help seemed a little easier than inventing sci-fi technology, so Sarah put her book aside, got on her computer, and logged on to the camp blog. Her friends would be happy to give her advice, but Sarah had to be careful how she asked for it. If Avery hadn't figured out the movie set sitch, Sarah didn't want her reading about it on the blog. Avery had turned out to be a lot nicer than she seemed at first. But Sarah still didn't want to hand over the ammo Avery could use to destroy Sarah's life.

She thought for a few minutes, then began to write.

Posted by: Sarah
Subject: Boy-Induced Insanity

I'm going crazy. Possibly take the "going" out of that last sentence. So I'm calling on the sisterhood for help. Here's the rundown.

I met a guy a few weeks ago. A cute—make that gorgeous—guy. He's great. He makes everything fun. And he's really into me. He notices things about me that I haven't even noticed about myself.

So you're probably all thinking, where's the problem, Sars? The problem is, this guy knows somebody who knows me. And this person knows something really embarrassing about me. Humiliating. Cringe-worthy.

I'm afraid if the guy finds out what the person knows, he'll think I'm too pathetic to even look at again.

What do I do?

Sarah's friends must have realized how desperate she was. She started getting responses almost right away.

Posted by: Jenna
Subject: Easy Solution

Your real problem is the person who knows this info about you. You obviously don't trust him/her. The easy solution—assassination. You won the game at camp, now it's time to move on to the real thing.

I did a little research for you, since as a crazy person, I wasn't sure you could do it yourself. I think the best way to go would be with an accident scenario. Arrange a private meeting with this person near a window (open, unscreened), bridge, stairwell, elevator shaft. Basically anyplace that has a convenient seventy-five-foot drop that ends on a hard surface. You see where this is going. A little push, then you start screaming about the horrible accident that just happened. There are lots of other methods if you don't like this one, but most of them involve some kind of equipment.

You can do it, Sars!

Killing Chace/Peter's sister. Somehow that didn't seem like the best idea . . . Besides, Avery was a fighter! Even though Sarah *had* turned out to be the top Assassin at camp during the summer, she didn't want to go mano a mano against Avery.

Sarah returned to the posts.

Posted by: Priya
Subject: It can't be that bad

Sarah. Sarah, Sarah, Sarah. Whatever this deep, dark humiliation is, it can't be that bad. I mean, you're Sarah!

My advice: Tell the guy whatever it is yourself. The insanity is coming from wondering if and when he's going to find out. And then what he's going to do. Just tell him. If he's as great as you say, he'll still like you. You're Sarah! If he doesn't, then you'll know. It will hurt. I'm not saying it won't. But you can cry and scream and we'll all call the guy really bad names, and then you can get on with your life (and start sleeping again).

Seriously, stop making yourself bonkers. Tell him.

Priya's advice made sense. It completely did. But when she tried to imagine standing in front of Chace and telling him how she'd felt so insecure around the Walla Walla campers—including his sister—that she'd borrowed her friend Natalie's life for herself, she started feeling nauseous.

And since just thinking about the scenario made her nauseous, she would probably actually throw up on Chace if she tried to follow Priya's advice and tell him the truth. Even if he could deal with her pathetic lie, would he really be able to deal with puked-on shoes?

Sarah wasn't willing to risk it. She moved on to the next post, hoping it would give her some advice that wouldn't lead to *more* humiliation.

Posted by: Chelsea
Subject: Move on

So this guy's great and gorgeous. I bet you can find another G&G with no problem. (I can't handle them *all* myself. =)) I say pick one that doesn't know the person that knows the secret. Problem solved.

Posted by: Sloan
Subject: Intuition

If you use your intuition you can find the answer within you yourself. Just hold your hands over your chest with your right palm over the back of your left hand, crossing your thumbs. Spread the fingers of both hands apart. Meditate on your decision while holding this position. It will heighten your intuition and increase contact with the spirit world.

There are all kinds of poses like this if anybody else needs help with anything. Just let me know.

Peace, love, and light.

Sarah didn't exactly like the idea of contact with the spirit world. It sounded scary. She was already borderline nutso. She didn't need to be dealing with ghosts, too.

The advice from Chelsea sounded good. Sarah composed an answer for the board.

Posted by: Sarah
Topic: Thanks

Thanks for all the help. You all deserve lifesaving badges!

I'm going with your advice, Chelsea, although I have to admit, it's going to take off several layers of skin—heart skin—to walk away from this guy. But like you said, I'll meet someone else.

I think I'll go try to take a nap. Hopefully now that I've made a decision I'll be able to sleep.

Natalie read the newest posts on the camp blog. It was like visiting her friends without having to show them her mouth. She could add to the blog without showing them her mouth, too. But if she posted, she'd get questions about what she was doing, and she wasn't sure she was ready for that. She didn't want to "talk" about Eli. She didn't have enough to say about him. He was nice. She liked his freckles. He was nice. He was really into models of all kinds. Actually, she didn't really want to give that detail. It didn't make him sound that interesting. And she was already back to nice. Which didn't sound that interesting, either. She couldn't say the thing she really liked about him—he had braces, so he didn't care about her braces. He didn't look at Nat like a freak.

Reading Sarah's posts had gotten Natalie thinking that Sarah had met her guy right around the same time Natalie had met Eli, about two weeks ago. And Sarah was already sooo emotional about him. So worried about what he would think of her. And so sad over letting him go.

It would be easy for Natalie to let Eli go. He was a casual friend. Nice. Cute. Kind of boring. Nice. Nat would miss feeling like a normal girl. But she wouldn't miss *Eli*. She wouldn't feel like she'd lost a layer of skin. Or maybe just the layer she was always pumicing off the bottom of her feet. Sarah was talking about layers of *heart* skin. Even thinking about heart skin sent a sympathy pain through Natalie's body.

An IM popped up on Natalie's screen.

<ModelGuy>: The weather is supposed to be awesome this weekend. I checked the five-day forecast. Wanna meet up in the park for sailing and lunch at the café?

The sound of whistling wind and a cry of "Land, ho!" came through her speakers. Natalie shook her head, but smiled. How could she say no? Eli was nice. With cute freckles. And more importantly, in life A.B. (After Braces), there weren't many options.

chapter
ELEVEN

"You might want to consider this mobile with the black-and-white graphics," the sales clerk at Petit Albert told Avery and her stepmother when they were out shopping on Thursday afternoon. "It's specifically designed to stimulate an infant's vision. The really terrific thing is, after two months, when your baby's vision starts to develop, you can change the elements on the mobile and introduce color." The clerk held up a not-at-all-cute yellow, black, and white triangle.

"We've decided we're not going to worry about stimulation in the baby's room," Avery told the clerk. "We want the nursery to be a beautiful place for the baby to chill."

The clerk gave Avery's stepmother a you're-not-letting-this-teenager-make-life-defining-choices-for-your-infant look. Elise smiled. "We're planning to have lots of stimulating objects for the baby in other parts of the house."

"You're aware, I'm sure, that a baby doesn't actually possess the concept of beauty. A baby loves contrasting colors. And I think this is quite elegant." The clerk gestured toward a black crib with a quilt of alternating black and white squares.

"I think we need to look at another store," Avery decided. Everything in the place had a geometric pattern and was black and white with maybe a little dash of another color.

The designs weren't even close to beautiful. And probably thousands and thousands and thousands of nurseries in Connecticut had something like them. Her dad and stepmother's baby should have something more special. The kid was going to be related to Avery, after all. It would be really embarrassing if it grew up to have bad taste.

"I can't go to one more store," Avery's stepmother said as they stepped back out into the main mall. "Except Ben and Jerry's." She pointed to the ice cream shop almost directly across from them. "I can and am going there." She started walking toward it like a magnet was pulling her there.

"Is this on the healthy-mother-healthy-baby eating plan?" Avery asked, following.

"You notice your father is already back to eating everything he wants," her stepmother answered. "Even though he was going to follow the plan in solidarity."

"I'll eat ice cream with you in solidarity," Avery offered. She didn't mind eating something decadent with her stepmother, because she, unlike Avery's mom, didn't talk the whole time they ate about the fat, carbs, and calories they were consuming and how much treadmill time it would take to "pay."

"Yes!" Her stepmother held out a fist for a bump, and Avery dutifully bumped it. Then they went inside.

There was something on Avery's mind. A question that nagged at her. *I'll do it when we sit down*, Avery promised herself as they got in line.

After I eat a few bites, she amended as they sat down at a little table with their ice cream.

What was her problem? She wanted to do this. Maybe she should have bought a card. Maybe that's why cards existed. Because it was too hard to actually *say* things. *Don't be a wuss. Just do it*, Avery ordered herself.

"Um, Elise—"

Her stepmother froze with her plastic spoon partway to her mouth. Probably because Avery had avoided using her name starting on day one.

"Yesterday, when we were talking . . ." Avery hesitated.

"When I was having my mental breakdown," Elise encouraged.

"Yeah. Well, you said that you didn't have any family here. And I thought that was weird. Because you live with family. You're married to my dad, and there's me, and Peter, even though he's pretty useless lately." Avery stabbed her ice cream a few times with her spoon. She liked it mushy. "So do you really feel like you have no family in Connecticut?"

"No. I really don't feel that way," Elise said very quickly. Too quickly.

Avery raised her eyebrows. "Why'd you say it then?"

Elise stared down at her cup of ice cream for a long moment, then she met Avery's gaze. "I want to feel like I live with my family here. And I'm an optimist. I think, in time, I *will* feel that way. But a lot of the time right now, I feel like your dad and I are a couple, and you and your dad and your brother are a family."

Avery wasn't going to try and talk her out of that. She could understand why Elise felt that way. That was pretty much how Avery felt. Or used to feel.

"That's going to change when the baby comes," Avery said. "Then you and dad and the baby will be the family. And Peter and I will be the, I don't know, the boarders." She hadn't planned to say that. It just came out. Like vomit.

"Sweetie, it's not going to be like that," Elise said.

"Things are already changing." Avery continued to spew, her voice ragged and cracking. "Dad didn't even read the comics on Sunday. And he didn't even notice when I hinted a million times about what I wanted for my birthday. And Peter. I don't even know why I act like Peter's in my family now. It's like I don't even have a brother anymore. He's always watching a movie. Even when he's not watching a movie, it seems like he's watching a movie in his head."

Avery felt her eyes sting with tears. She didn't want to cry. Not in Ben and Jerry's. In front of Elise. And the counter girl with bad acne.

"You know how I said in time I thought I'd start to feel like family with you and Peter? I'm actually feeling the family thing with you right now." Elise handed Avery a napkin. "And you know what? It felt like family when you talked me off the ledge yesterday."

Avery blew her nose, even though she thought blowing your nose in public was disgusting. But having fluid run out of your nose and down your face in public was more disgusting. "Your definition of family seems to involve a lot of crying," Avery muttered.

Elise laughed. "A lot of all kinds of emotion. Sometimes I've wondered if you and Peter are some kind of super-advanced robots, the way you're just polite and completely distant to me all the time."

"Well, I'm not sure about Peter . . ." Avery said.

"When I was your age, my brother basically lived in his room for three entire years. He never came out, never talked to any of the rest of us. We had to slide flat food under his door. Those plastic wrapped slices of cheese, mostly," Elise said. "When he came out, he had a beard and had somehow gotten engaged."

Avery laughed. Even though it was stupid. Actually, because it was stupid. Elise was actually kind of funny.

"Ready to go?" Elise asked.

Avery nodded. They stood up and tossed their paper ice cream cups and plastic spoons into the trash. "You should tell your dad you like it when he reads the comics," Elise said. "He would love that. You should also talk to him about how you're feeling about the family right now. How you feel like you're not that important to him and that he's not listening to you."

Clearly Elise had been listening hard.

"Can't I buy him a card?" Avery asked on the way out of the mall. "One of these conversations in a day is enough."

"It doesn't have to be today," Elise answered. "Maybe on Sunday. At brunch. I'm going to tell him to make at least *something* besides oatmeal. I'll eat oatmeal Monday through Saturday, but on Sunday, I want food food."

"If I talk to him at brunch, you'd be there, too," Avery said.

"Maybe the conversation could involve the whole family. If Peter's ready for something like that. You have to wait until people are ready." Elise lightly touched Avery's arm. "So what did you want for your birthday? I thought those belts I picked out were pretty cool."

"They were. Everything I got was great. But I'd been dropping major hint bombs about redecorating my room. It feels too little-girly," Avery answered. "I thought my dad got it, too, because I happened to see the paint chips and swatches in his briefcase."

"Happened to, huh?" Elise smiled. "Try hinting to *me* next time. I've pretty much become the designated gift buyer," Elise suggested. "Not that your dad doesn't need to listen to you." She pushed open one of the mall double doors and they stepped into the sunlight. "I've just had an inspiration!" she exclaimed. "What do you think of *your* curtains for the nursery? I love the little flowers."

"They'd be perfect for a baby. Even if it's a boy, we could do some stripes for the wallpaper or the bedding, to guy things up," Avery answered.

"Of course, if we take your curtains, we'd have to get you new ones. And then you'd probably need new bedding to go with them," Elise said.

"Maybe new carpet," Avery hinted.

"Oh, definitely new carpet," Elise agreed.

Brynn read Sarah's posts about the "guy" for about the twentieth time since they'd shown up on the camp blog yesterday. She gave a snort of disgust and shoved herself out of the chair in front of her computer. She began to pace as well as she could around her cluttered—truth, messy—room.

"She's talking about Chace. Of course she's talking about Chace," Brynn said aloud. Her family always teased her about her monologues, calling her a drama queen. But who cared? First, being a drama queen was a good thing, in her opinion. Second, if monologues were good enough for Hamlet and Lady Macbeth, they were good enough for her.

"I can't believe *Sarah* is worried about *Chace* finding out some secret about *her*," Brynn continued her rant. "Chace is evil. And Sarah is wonderful. Chace is devil spawn. And Sarah is awesome."

Okay, maybe that part was over the top, Brynn thought.

"What do I know for sure that Chace has done?"

she asked herself aloud. She stopped pacing. "I know for sure that he brought in a costume from outside and wore it." She nodded. "I know that. And it was against the rules."

"Yes it was against the rules," Brynn responded, as if she were Sarah. "But it didn't hurt anyone. It's hardly eeeevil."

"He hurt Lowell. He cheated Lowell out of a SAG voucher," she said as herself.

"There's no evidence to support that," Brynn-as-Sarah countered. "I thought we were dealing in certainties here. Or am I mistaken?"

"Point withdrawn," Brynn-as-Brynn answered. "Fact: Chace lied the day we met him when he said he was bringing me coffee for my migraine!"

Brynn-as-Sarah shook her head slowly. "I can't believe we're wasting the court's time with a petty accusation like that. Didn't you, only yesterday, tell Mr. Tollefson that you were late because you forgot to set the alarm, when you really overslept because you stayed up until three watching 10 *Things I Hate About You* for the seventeenth time?"

"I am not on trial here!" Brynn-as-Brynn snapped. But it was true, she had lied to Mr. Tollefson, and her lie was pretty much exactly the kind of lie Chace had told. A little excuse lie. "Chace and Sarah went to the movies without me! That was rude. And mean!" she burst out.

"Aha!" Brynn-as-Sarah exclaimed before taking a long dramatic pause. "Now we come to the heart of the matter. Ladies and gentlemen of the jury," (now

Brynn was playing a girl playing a prosecutor—they gave out Oscars for that, didn't they?) "this case isn't about facts. There is no proof for any but the smallest of the prosecution's accusations. What this case is about is hurt feelings and jealousy. The prosecutor is, in fact, deeply involved in the case. She is assuming that Chace and Sarah intentionally left her out. More than that, she is hurt that Sarah has wanted to spend time with a boy she likes instead of with the prosecutor. And the prosecutor is a little jealous of how Chace has managed to get a SAG voucher on his very first extra job."

Brynn walked over to her computer and sat down in front it. She quickly wrote an IM.

<BrynnWins>: I wrong. You right. I sorry. You okay?

<SarahSports>: I don't think I am.

<BrynnWins>: Awww. Chace is the guy, right?

<SarahSports>: Yes. I don't know what I'm going to do. Not true. I have to stay away from him.

<BrynnWins>: Why??? Just tell me, S. Maybe we can figure something out. Two heads.

<SarahSports>: Chace is Avery's twin. Using

a stage name.

<BrynnWins>: He shares DNA with Avery?? That explains a lot!!! So you're afraid he'll find out about the whole "Tad Maxwell's daughter" thing?

<SarahSports>: Yeah.

<BrynnWins>: You could push Avery out a window. Like Jenna said.

<SarahSports>: Heh. No. She isn't the total witch she first seemed like at camp.

<BrynnWins>: Maybe just ask her not to tell?

<SarahSports>: Don't think I trust her that much. Maybe that would make her tell. It's hard to know with Avery . . . Paranoia?

<BrynnWins>: Hmmm. We're still getting to know her angel/witch ratio.

<SarahSports>: I think I won't come to the set this weekend.

<BrynnWins>: Nooooo! Sars, don't quit. I'll run interference for you.

<SarahSports>: ??

<BrynnWins>: You don't want to be around Chace? It will be my job to keep the two of you apart. Okay?

<BrynnWins>: Okay?

<SarahSports>: Okay.

▲ ▲ ▲

"He's out there," Sarah told Brynn. She took another quick peek out the door of the women's dressing room. She'd only opened it a crack.

"Of course he is," Brynn answered.

They were only halfway through Saturday's extra duty, and Brynn had already been forced to do six interceptions on Chace, even though in the new crowd scene—set in 2040 this time—Sarah had managed to get assigned to a spot almost as far away from him as possible. She felt like she'd had one of those tracking devices installed under her skin. Chace seemed to be able to find her wherever she went.

"I'll go ask him if he's seen you," Brynn said. "Then he'll think he's wrong about you being in here, and you can just hang until we get called back to the set. I'll come get you. But I won't come back before then. It would make him suspicious."

"Thanks, Brynn," Sarah said.

How weird was it to be thanking someone for keeping the boy you liiiiked away from you?

"You need anything in your hideout? Bread, water, magazines?" Brynn asked.

"I'm good," Sarah told her.

"Okay, I'm gone." Brynn waved Sarah back from the door and disappeared.

Sarah sat down on one of the chairs, the neoprene of her costume making her sweat. Or maybe it was the stress of all the Chace avoidance. Everything in her wanted to be with him. And she kept forcing herself away. She wouldn't be surprised if her body snapped in half before the day was over.

chapter

TWELVE

Natalie didn't see Eli when she arrived at the Central Park model boat pond on Sunday, so she stood and watched the other boats slide across the surface.

A cry went up as a woman with the largest golden retriever Natalie had ever seen—clearly a mutant—struggled to keep her dog from leaping into the pond and destroying who knew how many hundreds of dollars worth of boats. She finally got him under control and hustled him off.

"Call the Dog Whisperer!" one of the sailors shouted after her.

Natalie wandered around the edge of the pond. It seemed like one of the sailboats was tracking her. She stopped. The boat stopped. She took a few steps. The boat followed. Was it Eli's? It was about the right size. She thought the stripe on the sail was the right color. But to her, a toy sailboat was a toy sailboat.

Except this toy sailboat had a teeny tiny

bouquet on it. Just three violets tied together with a purple ribbon.

"I'm pretty sure those are for you," a white-bearded, big-bellied man who looked way too much like Santa Claus told her.

Natalie knelt down. The boat glided right to the edge of the pond, and she saw that the bouquet had a little tag on it that said: "Natalie." She gently picked up the flowers, then turned around and started looking for Eli.

He stepped out from behind a tree, the boat remote in one hand and a bouquet of heart-shaped red and pink balloons in the other.

Wait, Natalie thought.

Eli bent down and picked up a large picnic basket, then hurried over to Natalie. He handed her the balloons. "Do you know what today is?" he asked.

Natalie wasn't sure of anything right now. "Sunday?" She wasn't even positive that was correct.

Eli laughed. "Yep, it's Sunday. It's also our two-week anniversary."

Oh, wait, wait, wait, Natalie thought.

But Eli didn't wait, wait, wait at all. Instead, he kissed Natalie on the cheek.

⛺ ⛺ ⛺

Sarah stared down the train tracks, impatient for Brynn's train to arrive. She was going to tell Brynn she was going home. Brynn deserved that. Then she was gone.

When she got on the train, she thought she'd be

able to handle the last day on set, at least with Brynn making sure to keep Chace away from her again. But she'd started feeling sicker and sicker the closer she'd gotten to Guilford. Make that the closer she'd gotten to seeing Chace. She couldn't handle another day like yesterday. She had to go home. And she would, as soon as she told Brynn.

Sarah felt the air begin to vibrate. The train was coming. Okay. Good. All she had to do was talk to Brynn for a minute, then Sarah would be buying her ticket home.

The train pulled into the station, and Sarah tried to watch every door at once as they whooshed open. Brynn, Brynn, Brynn, where was Brynn?

"Brynn!" she cried, rushing over to her friend.

"Hey!" Brynn called. "Ready for the last day—and the big wrap party in Manhattan?"

"No!" Sarah almost shouted.

"What?" Brynn asked.

"I'm sick. I realized I was sick on the train. I have to go home. Because I'm sick," Sarah explained in a rush.

Brynn studied Sarah for a minute, then shook her head. "You're not sick."

"Maybe not right this exact second," Sarah admitted. "But if I have to see Chace, I really will be. You'll have to ride with me in the ambulance to the emergency room."

"Sarah, I'll keep him away from you. Just the way I did yesterday," Brynn told her.

"I don't know if you can!" Sarah burst out. "He's

been IMing me, and calling me, and texting me. All last night. And he's already started this morning."

"What did you say to him?" Brynn asked.

"Nothing!" Sarah cried.

"Okay, good. That's good. So we'll just keep up the no-contact. We did it yesterday. We'll do it today." Brynn looped her arm around her friend's shoulders.

"That's not good enough!" Sarah shook Brynn's arm off, unable to stand still. "Because I'll still see him. And that's what's going to send me to the hospital!"

"Oh." Brynn nodded. "With layers of your heart ripped off."

"Exactly," Sarah answered. "This is the last day I'll probably ever see Chace, and if I see him, it will hurt too much."

"Look, Sarah. Maybe you made the wrong decision. Maybe instead of avoiding him, you should have just been honest and told—"

"Nooo!" Sarah wailed.

Brynn held both hands up in surrender. "Okay, okay. Never mind." She lowered her hands. "All I can say is, Chace really wanted to be with you yesterday. I should know."

"Which means Avery didn't say anything," Sarah said. "Unless it came up last night. Maybe it did. Maybe that's why he kept calling and texting and IMing. He just kept saying he had to talk to me. Maybe that's what he wanted to talk to me about." She grabbed Brynn's arm with both hands. "I need you to find out for me!"

"Without letting him know that I know Avery's

his sister." Brynn gently began prying Sarah's fingers away from her arm.

"Obviously. You can't tell him that. Just figure out a way to find out how close he is to Avery. How much they talk. Think of it as an acting assignment," Sarah suggested.

Brynn rolled her eyes. "How can I turn down an acting assignment?"

"Thank you, thank you, thank you!" Sarah exclaimed. "Oh, and you have to keep him away from me until you get the intel."

Brynn smiled. "You know me. I love a challenge."

▲ ▲ ▲

Operation Chase Chace Chace, Day Two, Brynn thought as she scanned the quad for her prey. Or acting partner, to see it another way.

There he was, playing hacky sack with the stand-in for the boy who had the part of Sam Quinn's son. Brynn decided to casually walk past in Chace's sightline. She was almost positive he'd ask her about Sarah. That way the whole conversation would seem like Chace's idea. Was she brilliant or what?

Brynn got into character. Which was Brynn, not thinking about Chace. As she strolled past the hacky sack game, she forced herself to concentrate on the backstory for Letshon, the 2040 character she'd come up with yesterday. That's what the Brynn character would be doing.

She must have done an excellent job acting like

her normal self, because she soon heard someone running up behind her. "Brynn, wassup?" Chace asked.

"Not much," Brynn said. Because while a lot was actually up with Brynn, not much was up with Brynn the character. "Sad it's the last day, but looking forward to the wrap party."

"So where's your partner in crime?" Chace used both hands to shove his hair away from his face.

Partner in crime. Did that have some double meaning? Did Chace suspect something? Was he trying to pump information out of her while she was trying to do the same to him?

"Sarah? She wasn't feeling that well. She went to the infirmary to get some aspirin," Brynn answered. It was always good to use as much truth as possible in acting. And Sarah *wasn't* feeling well. She probably could use an aspirin.

"Maybe I should go over there, see how she's doing," Chace said.

"She's probably already on her way back here to get in the wardrobe line," Brynn told him. "It doesn't take long to get aspirin. We should save her a place."

"Yeah. That'd be good," Chace answered.

After they joined the line, Brynn opened her backpack and started to paw through it. While she'd walked over from the train station, she'd come up with an awesome plan to get the info she needed.

"I'm going to massacre my brother!" she growled. "I keep telling him not to touch my stuff, and he took my iPod out of my backpack. I know it was him. He broke his. He's always breaking his stuff, then taking mine." She zipped the pack. "Do you have any brothers or sisters?"

"Huh?"

Huh? As in he hadn't been listening? Brynn had just given a great performance. "Brothers and sisters? You have any?" she asked, trying not to sound annoyed.

"A sister," Chace answered, looking around, for Sarah, Brynn figured.

"Does she mess with your stuff?" Brynn asked.

"Not really," Chace said. "We don't like that many of the same things."

That sounded good. Not liking the same things. Maybe Chace and Avery weren't close at all.

"Avery thinks if a movie's in black-and-white, it's defective," he added.

Brynn laughed, frantically trying to figure out what she should say next. "Uh, you should make her watch *Psycho*. It's so much scarier that the blood is black. At least I think so."

"Me too!" Chace said, his gray-green eyes brightening. "Did you know they used chocolate syrup for the blood?"

"Yeah. Isn't that cool?" Brynn answered. "Although do you think it made acting in the scene harder for Janet Leigh and Anthony Perkins? The smell of sweet, delicious chocolate while you're screaming or stabbing, depending if you're Janet or Anthony."

"That's the kind of acting challenge you have to deal with sometimes. Do you think it's harder to act in front of a crowd of people, or to act with a cameraman three feet away from you?" Chace asked.

"That's a tough one," Brynn admitted. "At least in the theater, the audience is in darkness. You don't see them until the lights come up at the end. It's easier to escape into the world of the play."

Off track! she told herself. "So would she do it? Your sister? Watch *Psycho*?" Brynn asked.

"Nah. She's wouldn't be into it. Just like I'm not into her horseback riding and the decorating shows she always has on. We used to hang more when we were little, but now I've got to stay focused," Chace said. "I read this article by an agent and it said only about one percent of people who want to be stars get to that level. I figure if I'm going to be in that one percent, I've got to be eating, drinking, and sleeping acting. I'm not even going to play tennis this summer. Half my friends are mad at me because I won't hang with them, but that's the way it's got to be right now."

Chace had handed her the intel Brynn needed. It really didn't sound like he and Avery sat around trading stories about what they did over the summer. So Sarah's secret would be safe.

The only weird thing was that Chace was soooo focused on his acting and Sarah was only doing the extra thing for fun. She'd probably never even do it again. She definitely didn't want to be a star.

So why was Chace so into Sarah? Brynn gave a mental shrug. Who could explain somebody in luuurve?

"You know what?" Brynn said. "I think I'll go

check on Sarah. She's taking way too long to deal with a headache or whatever little thing was wrong. Hold our place in line, okay?" she added before Chace could volunteer to go with her.

"Tell her I hope she's feeling better," Chace said.

Brynn smiled. *In about five minutes, Sarah is going to be feeling fantastic.*

"So I'm safe?" Sarah knew she'd already asked that question a bunch of times, but she had to ask it again.

"You're more than safe," Brynn told her. "You're golden. That boy really likes you. I think he'd like you even if he found out the Horrible Truth."

Sarah gasped.

"But he's not going to. Really," Brynn reassured her. "He and Avery don't talk much. And I doubt she would start telling him camp stories now. Why would she? It's not like we just got back."

"I wonder if he'll want to see me after we're done being extras," Sarah said. "We live sort of far apart."

"You'll never know unless you leave this bathroom," Brynn answered. "I'm going to go get in the wardrobe line. He's holding our place. Are you coming?"

Sarah looked at herself in the mirror. She'd bitten off all her lip gloss while she'd been waiting for Brynn to bring her the news. "One sec." She recoated her lips and considered putting on some perfume, but decided she was wearing enough. "Okay, let's go."

Brynn opened the door for Sarah with a flourish. *I'm going to see Chace! I'm going to see Chace!* The words skipped along with the fast beat of Sarah's heart. *Thereheistherheistherheis.* Her heart accelerated into the hummingbird-wing zone. She hoped Brynn wasn't really going to have to take her to the emergency room!

"Hi, Chace," she managed to say in a normal tone, as she and Brynn joined him in line.

"Sarah! I was trying to talk to you all day yesterday!" Chace exclaimed.

"Well, here I am." She threw her arms out to the sides, then pulled them close when she felt patches of pit sweat. Had he seen them?

"I wanted to know if you'd go with me to the wrap party tonight," Chace went on. "I know we're all going, but I wanted us to go together. I wanted you to be my date. If you want to."

Sarah didn't think she'd ever heard Chace sound uncertain before.

"That would be wonderful. Yes. Absolutely," Sarah told him. Out of the corner of her eye, she saw Brynn smiling.

"Good." Chace let out a long breath. "Yesterday it almost seemed like you were avoiding me."

chapter THIRTEEN

Natalie had a hard time swallowing even the small bite of brie and cracker she'd just taken. How could she not have noticed that Eli really liked her? And obviously—so obviously—he thought she liked him, too.

They had been IMing pretty much every day. And whenever Eli suggested they get together, Natalie said yes. They'd met up once after school this week for dessert at Serendipity. But they weren't boyfriend and girlfriend. Natalie was just trying him on. Like a pair of jeans. To see if they fit.

And boy, did this pair really not fit.

Natalie had to stop this. Now.

"Eli, this was so great of you. Thank you," Natalie said. That was the easy part. "But it seems like you're thinking of us as boyfriend and girl-friend . . ." She let her words trail off.

"You don't like me?" Eli asked, and she could see the hurt in his eyes.

"I like you!" Natalie assured him. "I do like

you. It's just . . . I don't think the two of us have much in common. Except our love of Serendipity's frozen hot chocolate."

"You didn't have fun at the train convention?"

"Uh . . ." Natalie nibbled on her lower lip. "Not really."

"You seemed like you were having fun," Eli protested.

"It felt like everyone was speaking a language I didn't understand," she tried to explain.

"It's like that for everyone at the beginning," Eli told her. "I can teach you. No problem."

"I don't think I want to learn," Natalie admitted.

"What about the boats? You had fun learning to sail the day we met, right?" Eli asked.

Natalie gripped her water bottle so hard it made a crunching sound. How much could she say? Should she say? "It was kind of fun."

"Why did you say yes when I asked you out again? You must have known model trains weren't your kind of thing," Eli said. "You must have known we didn't like the same stuff."

Natalie forced herself to put the water bottle down. She was going to demolish it if she didn't. "I got braces a couple days before I met you," she confessed.

Eli just looked at her. Clearly he didn't get it.

"I guess I thought since you had braces and I had braces, and no one without braces would be interested in someone with braces, it made sense for us to hang out," Natalie explained.

"Who cares who has braces?" Eli asked.

"No one at school can even look me in the face!" Natalie insisted.

"That guy right over there has braces and the girl he's with doesn't." Eli pointed to a couple Rollerblading by. "That girl has braces and no one is running in terror." He pointed to a girl selling hot pretzels who was laughing with a customer. "You can't be telling me you are the only one at your school who has braces?"

Natalie thought about it. Really thought about it. "My Spanish teacher has braces. But she's a teacher, so that doesn't really count." She thought a little more. "I think there's a guy in my chemistry class with braces. And there's a girl in math, too . . . I think . . ."

"You *think*! See, you don't know for sure, because it doesn't matter if she actually has braces or not," Eli pointed out.

Suddenly, people at her school who wore braces—at least a dozen just in her grade—flooded Natalie's mind. "You're right," she said slowly.

"Of course I'm right." Eli smiled.

"I'm really sorry, Eli. I didn't mean to use you. I just was so freaked out. And I guess I assumed you felt the same way I did about braces," Natalie said. "I thought we could be miserable together. But you weren't looking for misery."

"It's okay," Eli answered. "I guess I knew that we weren't exactly a great match. But I didn't care that much, because you're beautiful, even knocking off a few points for the braces. I'm shallow that way." He grinned.

"You're pretty cute, too. I love your freckles," Natalie told him. "Hey, just a thought, but what's your opinion on Rachel?"

"Great at wiring. Great at construction. Not so great at painting," Eli immediately answered.

"I don't mean as a train geek, geek," Natalie said. "I mean as a girl. Do you think she's pretty?"

Eli raised his eyebrows. "Rachel? I don't know. I feel like the last time I looked at her was when we were seven."

"I suggest you look again. Model skillz. And hot," Natalie said.

"Really? Rachel?"

"All I'm saying is think about it," Natalie told him. "So, friends?"

"I think we could be Serendipity friends," Eli agreed. "We could meet up for the occasional frozen hot chocolate and add more stuff to the list of all the things we don't have in common."

Natalie shook his hand. "Deal."

Chace dipped Sarah, sweeping her so low to the ground that the tips of her hair brushed the floor of Suzette's Garage. *Best night of my life!* Sarah thought as Chace pulled her back up and close to him. And the wrap party was just getting started.

"Want a soda?" he asked.

Sarah nodded.

Chace pointed to a deep purple sofa and Sarah happily sank down on the velvet to wait, taking in the scene. The studio had rented the whole massive NYC club. It belonged to the cast and crew for the night. There was a huge dance floor, a live band to back up anyone who wanted to sing karaoke, and way too much food.

Bloopers from the movie were playing on a loop on the many big screen TVs. Someone had added captions to them. Sarah didn't get all of them—inside jokes from times the extras weren't around. But she felt very TMZ when she did catch a reference.

The loop started to play again. How long did it take to get a couple sodas? There were four bars. Sarah checked the closest one. She didn't see Chace. She checked the next closest. No Chace. She had to stand up to check the third. No Chace. She looked up at the balcony to see the fourth—although there was no reason for him to be all the way up there. Didn't see him.

Maybe he made a pit stop in the bathroom first, she thought. The bathroom lines were always long. Although not as long for guys. Sarah sat down again. The velvet felt itchy and prickly. Why would you put a velvet sofa in a club? Clubs were always too hot, weren't they? She hadn't been to many others—well, any others. But with all the people and the dancing, they had to be.

Sarah watched the blooper loop all the way through again. Okay, it was crazy to keep sitting here.

Chace had probably run into Lowell or Temple and started talking. He probably thought she'd go find him. Probably.

She got up and started wandering through the crowd, making sure to look at every person she passed. Not Chace. Not Chace. Not Chace. Not Chace.

Chace. Chace in a shadowy corner with a girl.

Sarah moved a little closer. She couldn't get a good look at the girl. Chace was standing too close to her. But she could see that he held her wrist in one hand as he fingered one of the charms on her charm bracelet.

Sarah spun around. Her eyes blurry with unshed tears, she pushed her way through the crowd and ran straight into—

Avery.

Avery was here. That explained everything. Everything.

"You told him, didn't you!" Sarah demanded.

"Whoops, you almost made me spill my drink! Hi! I thought I might see you here. Is Brynn here, too?" Avery asked.

"That's what you say when you just ruined my life?" Sarah burst out.

"What are you talking about?" Avery's forehead crinkled.

"Let's talk outside. It's too loud in here." And too humiliating. Obviously Avery had told Chace the "Tad Maxwell's daughter" story. But that didn't mean everyone in the club had to hear it.

Sarah took Avery's arm and guided her through the crowd and out the door. "What is wrong with you?" Avery asked.

"You told your brother I lied about being Tad Maxwell's daughter!" Sarah accused. "Did he think it was funny how pathetic I was? Did you get a big laugh?"

"I'd forgotten about that." Avery took a step away from Sarah. "I have more interesting things to think about—and talk about—than you, Sarah."

"You're denying it?" Sarah's voice came out way too high.

"I said I didn't tell him," Avery said coolly. "Believe what you want. I'm going back to the party." And she did.

Sarah slumped against the side of the club.

▲   ▲   ▲

Brynn and Temple showed off some of their '50s dance moves to the electronica pulsing through the room. It didn't quite fit, but it was fun to try to make it.

Chace and Sarah had disappeared somewhere. Brynn had seen them dancing a while ago. They looked like the perfect couple, with Chace dipping Sarah, all romantic. Brynn missed hanging with Sarah at the party, but she'd played Cupid's assistant, and she was happy for her friend.

Brynn did a twirl transitioning out of the '50s-style dancing—and blinked. Was that—Yes. That was Natalie over there. She gave Nat a wave and hurried over. "You're here," she said, a grin spreading across her face. It had been way too long since she'd seen Nat.

"I'm here," Natalie mumbled, with a teensy, weensy smile.

All the phone calls Brynn had had with Natalie came rushing back. The one where Natalie had said she didn't need to be an extra. The one they didn't have where Natalie told Brynn about her new guy. The ones Brynn made to Natalie that Natalie never picked up—or returned.

"Are you mad at me or something?" she asked.

"Course not," Natalie muttered, her eyes widening.

Brynn listed off her reasons. "Because you barely smiled when you saw me. You don't seem to want to hang with me anymore. I told you I needed company on the set because Sarah got all caught up with this guy, but you—"

"Stop," Natalie said loudly and clearly.

Brynn thought she saw something flash in Natalie's mouth. Then Natalie smiled, a big, wide jack-o-lantern smile.

"You got braces!" Brynn exclaimed.

"And I think they did a partial brain removal at the same time," Natalie confessed. "I didn't want anyone to see them. That's why I backed out of being an extra."

"And smiled like this?" Brynn gave a skimpy little smile. "Why would you think anyone would care?"

Natalie laughed. "People keep asking me that." Her eyes darkened. "But some people do care. There are definitely other kids at school with braces. But my friends, they treated me like a freak. Hannah even said I was weird."

"Really? She said that to you?" Brynn demanded.

"No. I overheard her say it. I was hiding in a bathroom stall," Natalie said.

"Hiding?" Brynn repeated.

"Yeah, I'd hide until everyone was in the cafeteria, then I'd go to the library and eat," Natalie explained.

"If you did this while muttering and not smiling, I would say that the word weird kind of works for you, Nat," Brynn said gently.

Natalie's mouth dropped open. It finally sunk in. "I guess I should probably call Hannah when I get home."

"I think that's a good idea," Brynn agreed, looping one arm around Natalie's shoulders. "So what should we do now? Food? Dancing? Karaoke? I'm so glad you're here! I've missed my Natalie."

"I missed you, too," Natalie answered. "Let's go up to the balcony and—"

"I suppose you want to yell at me, too," someone said from behind them.

Brynn and Natalie turned around. Avery stood there, hands on her hips, chin high.

"Why would we want to yell at you?" Natalie asked.

Brynn had a pretty good idea. "You told your brother about—"

"No. I didn't," Avery interrupted. "Although I remembered I sent Peter a postcard from camp a while ago that said Tad Maxwell's daughter was in my bunk at Walla Walla. But that's it."

Avery turned away. Brynn scrambled around in front of her. "But he found out somehow? What did he say? Is Sarah all right?"

"I don't know. I was bored with being screeched at, so I left. She might still be outside," Avery answered.

"Let's go," Brynn said. She and Natalie started for the exit. Avery didn't move. "Come on, Ave. Come talk to her with us. She was just upset. She'll believe you if you say you didn't tell him now that she's calmed down."

"Fine." Avery gave an exasperated sigh. "One shriek and I'm out."

Brynn made sure she got out the door first. Sarah was propped up against the wall like a discarded mannequin. "Hi. I have Natalie and Avery with me. We want to talk, figure this out, okay?"

Sarah didn't say yes, but she didn't say no, and she didn't shriek, so Brynn led the others outside.

"Avery said that she did tell Chace—Peter— that Tad Maxwell's daughter was at camp with her," Brynn continued.

"I might have even told him that her name was Sarah Peyton," Avery admitted. "He's gotten so into acting and movies. It was the only thing I could think to write that he'd be remotely interested in. But I didn't tell him when the whole thing turned out to be . . . a mistake."

That was remarkably delicate of Avery, Brynn thought.

"But he ditched me," Sarah said, her voice flat. "One minute we were dancing, then poof, he was with some other girl. Why would he do that? When he asked me to be his date for the party, he seemed so excited."

"Well, nobody but camp people know about the *thing*," Natalie said. "So it can't be about that."

"You got braces," Avery suddenly said, as if she'd just noticed.

"Yeah," Natalie answered. "So what else could it be? What else could have changed his attitude so fast?" She, Brynn, and Sarah turned to Avery.

"I told you, I—" Avery began.

"I guess we're just thinking you know him better than anyone," Brynn said.

"Not lately. All he does is shut himself in his room and watch DVDs. Of black-and-white movies," Avery answered.

"When I was talking to him yesterday, he said he had to eat, drink, and sleep acting because that's what it takes to become a star," Brynn said. "For a minute, I wondered why he wanted a girlfriend at all. No offense, Sarah."

Sarah waved the comment away.

"Oh," Avery said.

"What?" Natalie asked.

"I think I see a connection. Maybe Peter wanted a girlfriend who could help him become a star," Avery explained.

"Like Tad Maxwell's daughter," Natalie said. And Natalie would know.

"But he zeroed in on Sarah right away. Like two seconds after she came on set he was already flirting with her. How did he know who she was?" asked Brynn.

"Don't forget, Sarah has been going to Walla Walla for a while. I must have pointed her out in a group picture at some point," Avery said.

"But weren't we saying he still thinks I'm Tad Maxwell's daughter?" Sarah asked. She straightened up. A good sign.

"Yeah. He should still want to be with her, then," Brynn agreed.

"This one time . . ." Natalie hesitated. "Okay, embarrassing story of my own. This one time, when I was eleven, this really crush-worthy boy who was about seventeen paid all this attention to me at a party I went to with my dad. I felt so grown-up and I thought my powers of flirtation were so on. But then Serena McAllen showed up, and he was suddenly all over her. And she's about eighty years old."

Natalie pulled in a deep breath. "Next day, I read in a tabloid about how this guy was working the party. First flattering Tad Maxwell's little girl, then moving on to bigger fish and wooing Serena McAllen, who happened to be about to make a comedy about a senior citizen falling in love with a high school guy."

"Awww, poor little girl, Nat," Brynn said.

"Maybe Chace is like that guy. Maybe he found somebody higher on the Hollywood food chain at the party," Natalie suggested. "Who was the other girl you saw Chace with?"

"I don't know," Sarah admitted, her voice soft and sad.

Brynn slapped her forehead. "You don't know, but I bet I do! I was at the table where they're making crepes, and I saw Kobie Armstrong, who plays Sam Quinn's son in our movie, hug this girl. He kept thanking her," Brynn told the others. "After they moved away from the table, somebody said that Zan always has her daughter help with casting teen roles, because she thinks teens know what other teens like."

"Director's daughter who helps with casting— and Zan is going to be casting a new movie next month—tops Tad Maxwell's daughter," Natalie said.

"I'm so stupid," Sarah moaned. "Why didn't I get it? I'm not eleven like Nat was. I even thought that it was weird that he picked me out of all the girls on the set, just walked up to me. But I didn't think . . . I just believed he thought I was special."

"You are special, Sarah. But that's not what Chace is interested in. He's just interested in whether someone has the connections that can help his career," Brynn told her. "And I believed he liked you, too. I believed it so much, I got a little jealous."

"We're going in," Avery announced. "If he's with

the director's daughter, I'll take care of it."

"What does that mean?" Sarah asked.

"It means you're not the only one I've got the goods on," Avery said. "I've lived with Peter a long time. Maybe I should go with the time he was hanging upside down on the jungle gym, then realized he had to go to the bathroom and couldn't remember how to get down. That's not an image you want of your boyfriend." She looked directly at Sarah. "Or maybe I'll tell her about his latest—when he made one of my friends think he was in love with her because he thought she could help him become a star."

Sarah scratched her head nervously. "Isn't that a little harsh? I mean, I'm touched that you'd stand up for me in that way, but you *are* his sister and all. You don't have to take my side."

Avery put her arm around Sarah's shoulders. "I may be his sister, but I'm also a member of the sister-hood. Peter needs to learn a lesson and this is the best way to teach him."

▲ ▲ ▲

Natalie saw herself and her friends projected all over the room on flat screen TVs as she, Brynn, Avery, and Sarah blasted out "Watch Me Shine" in front of the live band. She grinned, and watched her screen image grin back. It felt gooood!

A redheaded boy jumped up onstage with them for a minute. He sang a few lines, then grabbed Sarah's mike. "Zan just invited me to audition for her new movie!" he cried. He broke into a break dance. It was the worst break dance Natalie had ever seen, but the crowd went crazy with applause, anyway.

"Go, Lowell!" Brynn and Sarah shouted as he jumped off the stage.

Brynn nudged Sarah in the side with her elbow, then jerked her chin toward the crowd. Avery's brother was shoving his way toward the stage.

"What did you tell Zan Lazarus's daughter?" he yelled at his sister, his face red and sweaty. The girls could barely hear him over the roar of the crowd and their own singing.

Avery just waved at him, without stopping her singing.

He turned his attention to Sarah. "By the way, I found out you aren't really Tad Maxwell's daughter!" he shouted. "There are people here who have met her, and you're not her!"

"But *I* am!" Natalie called.

Chace's mouth dropped open.

She pointed to Sarah. "And this—this is one of Tad Maxwell's daughter's best friends!" Natalie started to wave at Chace along with Avery.

Then Sarah started to wave. Brynn began waving at Chace, too.

All four girls began dancing, working the wave into their moves, giving everything to the song. Natalie caught another glimpse of the four of them on one of the TV screens. *We do shine*, she thought. *Especially with the light bouncing off my braces!*

Chace opened his mouth as if he were about to say something. For a moment he stood there with his mouth agape. Eventually he closed it. He must have known. There wasn't anything he could say that would make a difference. So he turned on his heels and walked away. Quietly and alone.

Turn the page for a sneak preview of

camp CONFIDENTIAL

Politically In Correct

available soon!

chapter
PROLOGUE

Posted by: Natalie
Subject: oh. my. GAWD!

guys, you'll never guess who i just saw on
the nightly news! (brief sidebar—my mom has been
so busy with the gallery lately that her idea of
"quality time" these days is discussing current
events after thirty minutes of katie couric. insert
yawn here.) our very own dr. steve! apparently
camp walla walla is one of the first camps to "go
green" and he is planning this amazing festival to
open the summer season.

i know, some of you might be thinking,
"um . . . so what?" or "natalie, do you have ice
cream-related brain freeze again?" but wait . . . it
gets BETTER!!!

the president—as in the president of OUR
COUNTRY—is sending his daughter, tricia, to camp
walla walla! since, as everyone knows, he's our first
green president, he wants his daughter to participate
in the festival. isn't that INSANE?! we are going to be

sharing a bunk with the daughter of the leader of the free world! i don't think i've been this excited about camp in the history of forever. only two more days to go! =)

Posted by: Jenna
Subject: The prez's daughter? Fo realz?

Seriously?! The president's daughter is going to be at Camp Walla Walla?! You better not be pranking us, Nat. That's my job! Tee-hee.

Posted by: Chelsea
Subject: The reports are all true!

My parents saw the segment on the news, too! I am soooo psyched about meeting Tricia. Every time I see her on TV, she looks amazing. Great designer clothes. Perfect makeup. Precious mini-cavadoodle in her over-sized purse! Eek! I'm freaking out over here. To the point where I might faint. Must find a paper bag to breathe into. BRB.

Posted by: Sarah
Subject: Question

Do you think Tricia's bodyguard will have to share a bunk with us? That could be weird.

Posted by: Sloan
Subject: Facts about the First Daughter

I googled Tricia and here's what I found out.

1) Her favorite food is seedless red grapes.
2) She loves to read, especially about vampires.
3) She has an A- average and she's studying three languages.
4) Paris is the name of her cavadoodle.
5) She volunteers once a week at an organic food co-op, is vice president of her school's recycling club, and her favorite gym course is yoga.

Wow! I like her already. Can't wait to see all of you in a few days!

Posted by: Brynn
Subject: American Idol

Volunteers? A- average? Studies three languages? I'm impressed! Not too fond of red grapes, though. I mean, isn't everyone's favorite food pizza? Just sayin'.

Posted by: Natalie
Subject: can't wait

here's to a fantastic season at camp! see you all on sunday. yippee!!!!

chapter ONE

Late Sunday morning, Natalie Goode dumped two large, purple duffel bags on her twin-size bed and wiped her glistening forehead with the back of her hand. Even though she was never big on working up a sweat, she couldn't have been happier to finally arrive at Camp Walla Walla. Not only was she going to see all of her best friends again, but she'd also have the opportunity to get to know the president of the United States' daughter at "The Greenest Camp in America."

Truly, there was nothing cooler than that.

"Only two bags this summer, Nat? You're definitely slipping."

Natalie was still a little gun-shy about smiling since she got her braces, but she couldn't stop herself from breaking into a toothy grin at the sound of the familiar voice. She spun around and saw Sloan, decked out in a pair of canvas sneakers and a light green T-shirt.

"Shut up and give me a hug!" Natalie

grabbed Sloan and wrapped her arms around her friend tightly.

"Okay, okay. You're crushing me," Sloan said, her cheeks turning pink.

Natalie laughed and let go. "I'm sorry. I'm just excited to see you!"

"If that's how you greet me, I'm afraid of what you're going to do when our celebrity camper arrives," Sloan joked, as she rolled her suitcase over to the bed adjacent to Natalie's.

"You're forgetting who you're talking to. Celebrities don't freak me out the way they do everyone else. They're just average people like you and me."

No one was a stranger to the fact that Natalie's father was megastar Tad Maxwell, but sometimes Natalie felt the need to remind her friends that she wasn't a gossip-obsessed fame-monger.

"How is it possible that I already got stung by a bee?"

Natalie and Sloan smiled in unison when they saw their friend Chelsea walking into the cabin, holding back her blond hair and pointing at her neck. "Is it bad? Don't lie to me. I can take it."

"It's pretty standard for a bee sting, Chelse. Just red and puffy," Sloan answered.

"Well, I can't let the president's daughter see me this way. She'll think I'm a complete loser," Chelsea said with a sigh.

"Oh, stop it. You look great!" Natalie flung her arms around Chelsea and pulled her in close for a hug. "I've missed you!"

Chelsea stared over Natalie's shoulder at Sloan, confused. "Why is Natalie trying to squeeze me to death?"

"I haven't figured that out yet," Sloan replied, giggling.

"I'm just psyched to be here, that's all! Dr. Steve said on TV that the camp has a lot of new features, and this festival he mentioned sounds awesome, and there's a chance that the president's daughter will be staying in our bunk, and that the camp is growing, which means that maybe there will be a lot of new boys this year." Natalie paused for a second to catch her breath. "I'm rambling, aren't I?"

"Yes, you are. Now release me from your choke hold—you're going to kill me," Chelsea croaked.

Natalie chuckled as Chelsea wiggled out of her embrace. "I can't wait to see everyone at orientation."

Sloan glanced at her watch. "Won't be long now. Dr. Steve's expecting us all at the new rotunda building at noon."

"I heard it's powered by solar panels on the roof," Natalie said.

"Do they still have calamine lotion at the infirmary? Because I am in desperate need of some," Chelsea said while scratching at her neck.

"If they do, I bet it's organic," Sloan said with a wink.

Natalie was buzzing with such excitement that

she couldn't sit still at the orientation meeting. She was surrounded by more of her good friends who had been slowly arriving at camp all morning—Jenna, Priya, Brynn, and Sarah—and the new rotunda building was absolutely amazing. The solar panels on the ceiling were made of a translucent material, so everyone could look up and gaze at the white, puffy clouds that were moving slowly through the perfectly blue sky.

"First day of camp is such a rush," Jenna said as she retied one of her high-top sneakers.

"I wish Dr. Steve would get on with the show. We have so much to talk about!" said Priya.

"Never mind talking! Has anyone seen Tricia yet?" Chelsea said, her head pivoting back and forth as she checked out the crowd.

"Nope, not me," replied Sarah.

"I haven't, either," Brynn chimed in.

"Maybe she's in disguise!" Priya suggested.

Natalie chuckled, along with the rest of the girls. It was hard to imagine someone like Tricia bothering with li'l ol' Camp Walla Walla.

Priya crossed her arms over her chest. "Don't laugh. I saw it in a movie once."

"Whoa, check out the hottie over there," Brynn said, pointing to a spot a few rows ahead of them.

Natalie peered over the heads of the campers sitting in front of her and caught a glimpse of a posse of boys sitting to the left of them. A very good-looking, brown-haired, olive-skinned boy that she had never seen before was talking with David and Jordan.

"Okay, I have to say it," Sloan said with a wide grin. "Yuuuuum!"

Just as Natalie and the other girls burst out laughing, Dr. Steve stepped in front of the podium and tapped the microphone a few times to make sure it was on. Then he cleared his throat, causing some feedback to echo throughout the room. Natalie covered her ears and winced.

Well, that's one way to get everyone's attention.

"Sorry! Didn't mean for that to happen," Dr. Steve said in a flustered manner. He ran his fingers through his hair nervously and took a deep breath. "What I meant to say was: Welcome back to Camp Walla Walla, folks!"

Natalie clapped cheerfully with the rest of the campers. She scanned the crowd a bit more for familiar faces. Her eyes settled on Avery. What a relief it was not to feel stressed out by her anymore. Thank goodness that hatchet was buried.

"Now that we're one of the greenest camps in America, we are fully equipped to conserve energy and use only natural resources," Dr. Steve announced while members of the audience listened intently. "I'm sure all of you are going to like the improvements we've made."

"When is he going to get to the good stuff?" Priya whispered into Natalie's ear.

Natalie knew she was referring to Tricia, but Natalie was actually hoping Dr. Steve would talk more about the Green Festival, too. She was gradually going green at home and in school—she might have felt a little guilty if she was suddenly adding to her carbon footprint again.

"I'm also sure the word has spread that the president's daughter, Tricia, is coming to Camp Walla Walla," Dr. Steve said.

The audience erupted into wild applause. In fact, some girls jumped out of their chairs, shrieking like crazed fans.

"All right, settle down," Dr. Steve said with a laugh. "Tricia was supposed to be here today, but she was on a goodwill tour with her father and her flight out from London was canceled due to poor weather. So she's going to be delayed."

The shrieking girls immediately groaned and sat down in disappointment.

"In the mean time, I am putting together a group that will help me plan the Green Festival, a weekend-long event featuring live entertainment, fresh organic food, and eco-conscious vendors," Dr. Steve continued. "And, of course, the group will need a chairperson to lead them in the right direction."

"Wow, that sounds so cool," Sloan whispered to Natalie.

What was so unexpected, was that it sounded kind of cool to Natalie, too.

JUN 0 1 2010